"What are you thinking about?"

His gaze landed on her face. "Do you really want to know?"

Addison thought she saw a whisper of something inviting in Kellen's eyes. It was a look that said he wouldn't mind a kiss, and she caught her breath as he bent down toward her. For just a minute she felt like a young woman coming home from a date, her chest filled with the anticipation of a sweet first kiss with a promise of something more to come.

Addison quickly backed up.

She wondered what his mouth would taste like, how his lips might play on her own. It would be the height of stupidity to allow a kiss to take place between them.

Yet she was powerless to resist.

His mouth covered hers hungrily.

A five-star kiss in a five-star hotel, his mouth soft and suggestive on her lips, his scent, the feel of his warm hands on her flushed cheeks. There was a moment where Kellen increased the pressure, where he shifted just a little, and she felt as if they were both lost in the moment.

She returned his kiss with a hunger that belied her outward calm. Burying her face in his neck, Addison breathed a kiss there.

When the kiss ended, she resisted the urge to touch the place where his lips had been. Her heart was racing, and Addison could feel her blood rushing through her veins. She was falling for Kellen.

Books by Jacquelin Thomas

Harlequin Kimani Romance

The Pastor's Woman
Teach Me Tonight
Chocolate Goodies
You and I
Case of Desire
Five Star Attraction
Five Star Temptation
Legal Attraction
Five Star Romance
Five Star Seduction
Styles of Seduction
Wrangling Wes
Five Star Desire

Harlequin
Kimani Arabesque

Treasures of the Heart
To Mom, With Love
Stolen Hearts
With a Song in my Heart
Undeniably Yours
Love's Miracle
Family Ties
Cupid's Arrow
Someone Like You
Forever Always
A Resolution of Love
Hidden Blessings

Kimani New Spirit

Saved in the City
Soul Journey
A Change is Gonna Come
The Prodigal Husband

JACQUELIN THOMAS

is an award-winning, bestselling author with more than fifty-five books in print. When not writing, she is busy catching up on her reading, attending sporting events and spoiling her grandchildren. Jacquelin and her family live in North Carolina.

FIVE STAR DESIRE

JACQUELIN THOMAS

HARLEQUIN® KIMANI™ ROMANCE

Bernard, you are my best friend and the love of my life. As always, thank you for being my #1 fan and supporter.

Recycling programs for this product may not exist in your area.

ISBN-13: 978-0-373-86362-4

FIVE STAR DESIRE

Copyright © 2014 by Jacquelin Thomas

For questions and comments about the quality of this book please contact us at CustomerService@Harlequin.com.

Printed in U.S.A.

Dear Reader,

Five Star Desire is the fifth book in the Alexanders of Beverly Hills series. This story features Kellen, the youngest son of Malcolm and Barbara Alexander. Kellen believes he is ready to tackle the Special Projects Director position. However, he finds that someone else has already been given the job and he's slated for a lesser role in his father's company. When Kellen discovers that Addison Evans is his boss, the two clash in the beginning, but eventually things between them turn passionate, as he is determined to find his happily ever after with her.

Best,

Jacquelin

Chapter 1

Kellen Alexander strolled briskly into the elegant living room of his parents' Mediterranean-style home in Pacific Palisades.

"Good to have you home for good, little brother," Dreyden said when Kellen greeted him at the front door.

"It's good to be here. Hey, I've been thinking that you need a roommate." Kellen loved living in Atlanta, but he was enjoying his reunion. At the age of twenty-six, he had just recently completed his master's degree in architectural engineering and was thrilled to be done with school and back in California with his family.

Dreyden chuckled. "I don't think so. I actually enjoy living alone."

"C'mon…it's not like I'll be around much," Kellen uttered with a sly smile. "I've got a lot of catching up to do with the ladies."

Kellen toured the main floor, in search of the rest of his family. He took the stairs to the second floor. His oldest brother, Ari, was the father of three children—a pair of fraternal twins, one a boy and the other a girl, and another son. He was with his wife, Natalia, in one of the spare bedrooms, trying to get the twins, Christian and Crystal, to settle down. Kellen had seen their brother, Joshua, occupied in the family room playing a game on an iPad. Hearing the sound of laughter, Kellen went back downstairs where he found his brother Blaze and wife, Livi, settling down in the family room.

Kellen walked to the kitchen, where his mother and sisters were busy preparing dinner.

"Get out of here, little brother," Sage ordered, pushing him away.

"I see you're still bossy," he responded with a laugh.

"And you're still a pest," Zaire interjected. "Go play guest of honor. We got this."

They were trying to be secretive about the menu, but Kellen knew they were up to something. He had a feeling they were cooking up something special.

Malcolm Alexander cleared his throat, commanding everyone's attention. "Everybody come in here."

Kellen ventured into the family room with the others. "What's going on?" he asked.

"Dad's about to make a speech," Sage whispered as she stood beside him.

"I feel so blessed to be surrounded by my children and their families," Malcolm stated. "I'm so proud of all of you."

Malcolm was the heir of the late Robert DePaul's multimillion-dollar estate and chain of luxury hotel and spa resorts. Kellen was glad to see that his father had finally made peace with the discovery that his parents had kept the truth of his biological father a secret from him. For the majority of his life, Malcolm had grown up believing that Theodore Alexander was his father, but his mother had taken the truth to her grave.

"We love you, Daddy," Zaire said.

He smiled. "I love all of you, as well. Today we are here to celebrate Kellen and his accomplishment. He graduated with honors." Malcolm turned to him. "Your mother and I are very proud of you. There was a moment when we weren't sure you were going to attend college, much less graduate school…" He suddenly broke into a grin. "But I'm happy to say that you proved us wrong."

"I admit I partied a lot when I first went off to college," Kellen confessed with a tiny smile, "but when you made me come home for a semester when I was a freshman—it changed my perspective, Dad. I didn't see it back then, but it was probably the best thing you could've done for me." He wrapped an arm around his mother. "I really appreciate your support and all those late-night talks, Mom."

Barbara placed a loving hand to his cheek. "Your father is right. We are very proud of you."

"Kellen, we're all so proud of you, too," Zaire interjected without preamble. "Now can we eat? I'm starving."

Laughter rang out around the room filled with his family.

"C'mon," Sage uttered. "She's eating for two. When I was pregnant with Honor, all I could think about was food."

Her husband, Ryan, nodded in agreement.

"Zaire, you don't have to wait any longer, sweetie. Dinner's ready," Barbara announced when she returned from the kitchen.

Everyone followed her to the formal dining room.

Kellen not only felt good about being home, he was home for good and ready to take on the world—more specifically the Special Projects Director position for Alexander-DePaul Design Group. Kellen had had his eye on the employment opportunity since it posted. He was confident his father would give him the job.

"I see you made all of my favorites," Kellen stated. "Thanks, Mom. I have to tell you that I've really missed your homemade biscuits, fried catfish and especially your collard greens."

"Have you learned to cook anything outside of hot dogs and hamburgers?" Zaire inquired.

Kellen nodded. "I'm pretty good with breakfast foods. I can make some mean omelets."

"That sounds good," his younger sister said. "You can make me one for breakfast tomorrow morning."

"Zaire, do you ever stay at your house?" he asked with a chuckle.

"Yeah, but when my husband's out of town, I usually stay out here. Tyrese is leaving tonight for New York."

Some unknown assailant had attacked Zaire over a year ago, and now that she was pregnant, her husband preferred that she stay with her parents whenever he was out of town. There were a few times when Franklin, the loyal and trusted head of security his parents had inherited after Robert's death, stayed with her when she chose to remain home.

Seated at the dining room table, Kellen let his gaze wander around, landing on his parents and his siblings, before he sampled his food. "Mom…superb…"

Barbara smiled. "Thank you, dear."

His gaze landed on Dreyden. Silently, he noted that his brother had lost weight in a relatively short period of time. When Dreyden had surprised him in Atlanta just a couple of months ago, he'd looked fine.

"Dreyden, what's up with you?" Kellen inquired in a low voice after everyone settled down in the large family room after dinner. "I couldn't help but notice that you didn't eat much at dinner. To be honest, you don't look like you're feeling well."

"I've just been really tired lately," his brother responded with a slight shrug. "We just finished tax season, so I won't be working late as much."

"Why don't you take a vacation?" Kellen suggested "Go somewhere exotic."

Dreyden smiled. "I've been thinking about that myself. Maybe I'll see a travel agent next week and plan a trip."

"Do it," he encouraged. "You need a break away from work." Kellen was worried about his brother. He had never seen him look so pale or exhausted.

He rose to his feet.

"Where are you going?" Dreyden asked.

"I need to talk to Dad about the Special Projects Director position at the Alexander-DePaul Design Group. I applied as soon as it became open, but I haven't heard anything from human resources."

"Why don't you just enjoy being with the family, Kellen?" his brother suggested. "Think about work tomorrow."

"I'm excited, Dreyden… I really want this job. I've been waiting on something like this since before I graduated."

"I can see that, but just give it a couple of days. It's better to get the job based on your own merits and not because of your last name."

"I've spent all of this time in school so that I can prepare myself for this position," Kellen stated. "I've earned it."

"Hello, everybody."

Kellen turned around to find Harold DePaul standing in the doorway with a young woman he assumed was his fiancée, Amy. He knew that the couple had met at Blaze and Livi's wedding. Amy and Livi were close friends. "Harold, it's good to see you."

Harold and Amy were getting married in a couple of weeks. Kellen was initially surprised that he was engaged to an African American woman—especially after the way he reacted when his uncle left everything to his biological son—Malcolm Alexander. Kellen thought him a racist because of his initial reaction concerning his uncle's relationship with an African American woman. However, he and many of the DePaul relatives had come to look past skin color. "Congratulations on your surviving grad school. I bought you a gift."

"Thank you."

He and Amy moved on to talk with Barbara and Malcolm.

"Harold looks very happy," Zaire whispered.

Kellen agreed. "I never expected those two to hook up, but I can tell that they are crazy over one another. Talk about irony."

"I'm glad he's found someone," Zaire responded. "William's illness has been very hard on him."

"I can't imagine losing a brother…or a sister."

"I know."

Just then Livi walked into the room and made her way over to Harold and Amy. "Hey, you two…I'm glad you made it."

Kellen walked over to his father and said, "Dad, I applied for the Special Projects Director position a couple of weeks ago. I think the job is perfect for me, but I didn't get an interview for it. I did have a telephone interview with talent acquisitions, but it was for another position. Do you know what happened? I think they made a mistake."

"Son, there was no mistake," Malcolm said. "The director position has already been filled. Someone in-house was promoted. However, the architectural engineer position is yours. You'll start in a couple of weeks."

A shred of disappointment snaked down Kellen's spine. "I really wanted the special projects position. I feel I'm qualified for management."

"The person selected was more qualified for the position. You don't have seven-plus years in experience."

"I'm your son. Surely, you can override the decision to hire someone else."

Malcolm met his son's gaze. "What would you have me do, Kellen?"

"I have all of this education and you want me to work in a position that—"

"Let me stop you right there, son," Malcolm quickly interjected as he held up his hand. "Kellen, you do have the education, but you are lacking when it comes to hands-on experience. There is nothing wrong with starting in an entry-level position and working your way up."

Exasperated, Kellen argued, "Ari, Blaze and Sage didn't have to do anything like that. As for experience, I've interned and worked with the largest architectural firm in Atlanta."

"They didn't just come to their positions with education —they also came with years of work experience."

"I can't believe this," Kellen uttered in frustration.

"Honey, you can't expect your father to just *give* you a position," Barbara remarked blandly. "You have to earn it in the same manner as everyone else."

"Dad can do whatever he wants," Kellen responded. "The Alexander-DePaul Design Group is *his* company."

"You are not ready, son." His father gave him a reassuring smile. "Starting in an entry-level position is what you can expect from any company. It's not a bad place to be—the salary is competitive and you will be able to work on some exciting projects."

Kellen did not respond. He had come to Los Angeles fully expecting to be awarded the position. It had never occurred to him that his father would not give him the job.

"Dad's right, little brother," Dreyden interjected.

"You have your own firm and Zaire started her own company. Maybe I should do my own thing."

"You can do that, Kellen, but what real experience do you have?" Dreyden questioned. "What can you really offer a client coming to you?"

There was tightening around his mouth, but he didn't speak.

"I know this isn't what you want to hear, but it's what you need to hear. Learn your craft and then move up."

"Why does everyone think I'm so incompetent?"

Dreyden released a small sigh. "I don't think of you as incompetent, Kellen. You're impulsive and you want things to happen immediately."

"I can't deny that," Kellen stated.

"No point. I know you, little brother."

"I'm ambitious."

"There's nothing wrong with being ambitious," Dreyden said. "You need to recognize that your position is not exactly an entry-level one. You should be thankful because you could have ended up in the mail room."

"I do have a job and I am grateful for that. It's not exactly on the management track, but I guess I'll have my chance to impress my new boss in a couple of weeks."

Wisps of cirrus clouds played peekaboo with the early June sun. A steady wind, blowing in from the east, brought warming temperatures, and Addison Evans was looking forward to the summer. But for now, she needed to complete preparations for her new hires that were starting today.

She paced back and forth in her office. Why was she

so nervous? Kellen Alexander was just another employee. He was on *her* team. The fact that she was anticipating his arrival with such emotion came as a complete surprise.

"You're going to wear a hole in the rug," her assistant said. She walked into the office with a stack of documents. "This is what you've been waiting for. They arrived late yesterday after you'd gone home."

"Thank you, Devin."

"I have everything set up in the conference room for the new-hire orientation. Samantha from human resources should be arriving any moment. She called from the car."

"Great," Addison murmured. "Thanks for getting everything ready."

She sat down at her desk. "Let me know when the new hires arrive."

"Will do," Devin responded with a smile.

Kellen was the first to arrive.

"I'm Addison Evans." She smiled and extended her hand, which quickly disappeared into his large one. She made a point of keeping her grip firm and looking Kellen in the eye, a habit she'd acquired early in her career, and one that had always alerted her about what kind of man she was dealing with. "Welcome aboard."

"Thank you," he responded politely.

Kellen held her gaze and didn't seem surprised by the firmness of her grip. More important, he didn't try to grind her hand into dust with his superior strength.

Both marks in his favor.

Addison studied him, poised there so straight and tall in his sharply tailored, black, designer business suit. He was devastatingly handsome, but she crushed that thought as soon as it entered her mind. His dark-eyed gaze made the already hot day sizzle.

She forced herself to look away from Kellen. The man

had broad shoulders, slender hips and long legs that would easily turn a woman's head in his direction. Addison released a soft breath of air before turning her attention back to him.

He was easily the sexiest man she had ever met, but it wasn't just his looks that attracted her to him; it was the mystery and the intrigue that she found intoxicating.

She could not read him.

Kellen was smiling, but she silently noted that his smile did not quite reach his eyes. Addison had heard that Kellen was reputed to be very personable; however, she was not seeing this side of him at the moment.

"Where would you like me to sit?" he asked her.

She tore her gaze away and concentrated on his question. "Your office is two doors down. I'll have someone take you there after a brief orientation." Addison resumed control of her emotions. "I'll walk you to the conference room. I have two other employees starting today, as well."

"Great," Kellen murmured.

She stole a peek at him. He did not look as if he really wanted to be there.

"How long have you worked here?" he asked suddenly.

"I've been with ADDG for almost five years. I interned here during grad school and was hired permanently after I graduated."

"Where did you attend college?"

"Stanford," Addison responded. "Here we are," she said with a soft sigh of relief. "Your orientation will last until noon. We have a welcome lunch planned for one o'clock."

Addison walked briskly away from the conference room longing for the safety of her office. She was far too aware of Kellen as a sexy man, when she needed to look at him objectively like an employee. Still, it was hard to stay objective when he focused those gorgeous gray eyes on her, when the clean male scent of him eddied in the air around her and his energy filled every corner of the room.

She had to find a way to block out her intense awareness of this man.

Kellen had not expected to be struck down by Addison's beauty. The image formed in his mind was of a "plain Jane" type. Instead, her features were classic. Addison had high cheekbones that emphasized the slenderness of her face and her straight, perfect nose. She had a generous mouth, which he found incredibly sexy and her lips inviting.

She looked of average height; her curvaceous figure covered in a navy pencil skirt and jacket. Not a hair was out of place. Kellen admired the healthy glow of her butternut complexion.

While in her office, he glimpsed the many awards and accolades Addison had received throughout her career. Combined with the conservative navy suit she wore, he got the message. This woman was smart, dedicated and professional.

She had thrown him completely off guard. Kellen mentally shook himself and forced himself to pay attention to the human resources rep who explained the benefits of being an Alexander-DePaul employee.

Later, a walk through the open workstations revealed collaboration in action, which excited Kellen. He couldn't wait to get started on his first project. He intended to impress Addison with his skill. Kellen noted there were groups of associates gathered in one area or another throughout. Although he had group projects during his college years, he preferred to work solo when it came to a project.

"ADDG employees participate in a wide variety of activities—from fun to philanthropic—the annual golf tournaments, charity fundraisers and local office parties, just to name a few," the HR rep stated.

Afterward, Kellen joined the rest of the associates in a large area he assumed was the break room. For just a moment Kellen gazed at Addison, observing her as she interacted with her staff. She was a natural beauty, a woman comfortable in her own skin. Normally, when he glimpsed into the eyes of the women he came into contact with, he saw a hint of vulnerability in the depths of their eyes, but not in Addison's gaze. She obviously didn't need anybody to rescue her and besides, that wasn't his role here. Kellen knew without a doubt that she could stand her ground and hold her own against just about anybody.

"So what do you think?" she asked when she joined him by a table laden with food.

"I notice that everyone seems to work in teams. Collaboration seems to be the theme throughout."

"Collaboration means teamwork, and our integrative approach to project design is apparent in our staff relationships. Working with a variety of different professionals who share a common goal allows us to enjoy what we do and celebrate the satisfaction that comes from a job well-done."

"I tend to work better alone."

She looked up at him, meeting his gaze straight on. "You may feel this way now, but after you've worked on a few projects, I think you'll feel different."

Kellen disagreed, but did not vocalize his thoughts. "So what are some of the new projects your teams are working on?"

"ADDG took the lead on an exciting project in Denver," Addison stated. "We are designing a new ski resort. The building is going to be a replacement for the preexisting Hummingbird Lodge. In just under a year of design time, we are on target to bring the plans through the necessary variance and permitting phases and to completion."

"Sounds like an exciting project," Kellen admitted.

"Your job will entail developing structural renderings starting from conceptual to detailed design stage using 3D AutoCAD and Personal Development Management System."

He patted the backpack on his right shoulder. "I can't wait to get started."

Their eyes met and held.

She released a soft sigh, although he couldn't tell if the sigh was of relief or apprehension. "I'm certainly glad to hear that," Addison replied as she headed back toward the door. "I have to get to a meeting, but I'll check on you later."

Her steps were brisk and abrupt, almost as if she couldn't wait to get away from him. Kellen reminded himself that no matter how beautiful she was, Addison Evans was a mystery he definitely didn't need to explore.

Kellen carried with him an energy that seemed to pulse in the air around him, an energy that seductively drew her to him. Addison escaped into a conference room. But it was the way he stood, his head cocked to one side, an air of confidence about him which drew her like a moth to a flame. Maybe it was because she'd isolated herself for the past six months that Kellen touched a chord inside her.

She checked her watch.

Her meeting wasn't scheduled to start for another ten minutes, but she needed time to regain her senses.

Addison cast her gaze outside the window, where a light breeze stirred the trees. She always loved the spring season, before the summer heat tightened its grip on Los Angeles.

As she heard the door open and then close, her thoughts snapped back to work.

Members of upper-level management slowly filled the room. Addison turned her attention to the meeting agenda.

Reluctantly, her thoughts traveled back to Kellen. When his gaze landed on her, he seemed to be trying to look inside her soul, which is what prompted Addison to break eye contact with him and leave so abruptly. It was really ridiculous, the kind of tension his very presence wrought inside her. She was extremely aware of Kellen's maleness, when she needed to look at him as just another employee.

She didn't know why, but she had a feeling her life was about to change dramatically. Addison just wasn't sure if it would change for the good or the bad.

Chapter 2

Barbara walked outside to the patio where Kellen sat staring out at the picturesque landscape of the backyard and Olympic-size pool.

Feeling his mother's presence, he glanced up but said nothing.

"How was your first day at ADDG? You got in so late last night, I didn't get a chance to talk to you."

"Spent most of the day in orientation," Kellen responded drily. "I was able to get my office set up. I unpacked all of my books and magazines. I guess you could say that it was a good first day."

She sat in the empty lounge chair beside him. "Honey, I know you're disappointed about the management position, but your father made the right decision."

He gave her a sidelong look. "Somehow I figured you would agree with him."

She seemed taken aback by his response. "What is that supposed to mean?"

"Exactly what I just said," Kellen responded. He was careful not to sound disrespectful. "Mom, you rarely disagree with Dad over anything. So this doesn't surprise me that you'd side with him on this, too. Allies must present a united front, after all."

"Son, I'm not siding with anyone," Barbara stated. "In case you have forgotten, I've been in business for a while. If the decision had been mine to make—I would've made the same one."

"I've done everything I could to earn your trust." Kellen sighed in resignation. "What else do I need to do?"

"Nothing," she responded.

Barbara's warm brown eyes bored into his as she folded her hands in her lap—hands that were now adorned with a new wedding set. "This is not about trust, Kellen. This is a business decision and not a personal one. The fact that you haven't realized this confirms that you are not ready for such a position."

Kellen's mouth tightened in response. He glanced over at the ring on his mother's finger and said, "Blaze and I helped Dad pick that ring for you. I knew how much you loved emerald-cut diamonds."

She smiled. "I figured as much. Malcolm would've just picked something more extravagant."

"The one he had in mind was nice, but I told him that you wouldn't like it."

She reached over and gave his hand a gentle squeeze. "Son, keep an open mind. Learn the ropes and—"

"And maybe one day my chance will come," Kellen finished for her. He rose to his feet. *"Got it."*

"Don't you dare walk away from me, young man."

He turned to face his mother. "I'm not trying to be disrespectful, but I just don't have anything else to say."

Barbara merely raised an elegant eyebrow. "Fine," she responded firmly. "Then we don't need to discuss this anymore. It is what it is and you will have to adjust. Kellen, I know that you will because you are your father's son."

He glared at her, and she stared him down.

Addison met her best friend, Tia Browning, for dinner at the Cheesecake Factory in Beverly Hills. She had called her a week ago to tell her about the new position.

Dressed in a fashionable red-and-black pantsuit, Tia stood outside the restaurant waiting for her to cross the street. She switched her red leather tote from her left shoulder to her right.

"Hey, lady," Addison greeted her with a smile.

They embraced.

"Congratulations on your promotion to director," Tia said. "Girl, I'm so happy for you."

Addison broke into a grin. "Thank you. I have to confess that I didn't really think I'd get the job."

"Dinner's on me tonight," Tia stated. "I just got a huge bonus from work so we're celebrating."

"A bonus. Congratulations to you."

They were seated a few minutes later.

"I'm really excited about this new role," Addison stated as she picked up her menu. "The only thing I'm a little nervous about is that a member of the Alexander family is working under me."

"Really?" Tia pushed her menu to the side and leaned forward. "Which one?"

"Kellen," she responded. "He's the youngest son."

A waitress who identified herself as Paula greeted them warmly as she pulled out a pen and paper to take their drink selections.

When she walked away, Tia continued their conversation. "I read somewhere that he was away at college on the East Coast."

Addison picked up her menu. "He graduated last June and now he wants to join the family business."

"Are you going to be able to concentrate with such a gorgeous man like that around? Girl, I have to tell you— that is one good-looking family."

She chuckled. "He's going to be my employee, Tia. Besides, I'm five years older than him."

Paula reappeared with drinks for them. After setting them down on the table, she pulled out a pen and pad to write down their orders.

She disappeared around a corner and into a nearby wait station.

Tia took a sip of her wine. "I don't know if I could do it."

Addison laughed. "Regardless of how handsome he is, I'm not at all interested in mixing my love life with my business. You know that only leads to trouble."

"There are quite a few workplace romances that work out."

"I don't know of any."

"Yeah, you say that now…"

"I'm serious. I don't want to deal with any drama in the office if things don't work out. It's not professional, either."

"I don't know, girlfriend. Kellen Alexander looks exactly like your type."

"He may look like my type, but I'm not letting him get anywhere near me outside of work. I intend to focus on my job."

"Tell me that after you've worked with him for about three months," Tia said with a grin.

"There's a fine line between romance and sexual harassment," Addison stated.

"I doubt that Kellen is going to consider suing you."

She took a sip of her iced tea. "I'm not taking any chances."

"Like I said," Tia uttered, placing her napkin across her lap as their food arrived. "Three months from now, we'll see if you feel the same way."

"I was once told that I'd never be CEO of a major corporation because I didn't go for the jugular," Addison stated. "At the time, I took that to mean I wasn't tough enough, that I didn't have what it took to play the power games at any cost. Well, he was right at the time. Other things were equally important to me and I did not want to spend my life—every waking moment—thinking about business and the power games I would have to play to make it in the big leagues. Then my mother died and everything changed for me. Tia, I'm not about to let Kellen Alexander destroy all the hard work it took to get where I am."

Kellen was still upset over the job situation, and for the moment, he did not want to be anywhere near his parents. However, it was unavoidable because he was living in their house. This morning, he purposely stayed in his room until he knew they were gone. He knew that his parents religiously went on an early-morning stroll daily.

He was surprised to see Zaire seated at the breakfast table when he entered the kitchen. Kellen had no idea that his sister was there. He didn't have dinner at home last night and had stayed out until he was sure his parents had retired for the evening.

"Good morning," she said brightly.

"What's so good about it?" he grumbled as he dropped down in the seat across from her. "What are you doing here, anyway? Don't you have a house of your own? I know your husband is back in town. I talked to him last night."

"What's wrong with you?" Zaire asked, wearing a frown on her face. "I know you're not a morning person, but you're usually not so snappy. As for why I'm here— Mom and I are going shopping for the nursery."

"I'm sorry," Kellen responded. "I didn't mean to snap at you like that. I'm just in a bad mood." He and Zaire had shared an apartment while they were in grad school. She graduated a couple of years before him and decided to start a business of her own. She and Dreyden were the only two of his siblings that opted not to work in the family business.

"Clearly." Zaire poured a glass of orange juice and then took a sip. "Why don't you tell me what's going on with you?"

"You know how badly I wanted the Special Projects Director position. Well, Dad gave it to someone else."

She wiped her mouth on the edge of her napkin. "I told you that might happen, Kellen."

"I really didn't think Dad would do that to me."

Zaire passed him the pitcher of orange juice. "You really shouldn't take this so personally."

"I can't help it," he responded as he poured the orange liquid into a glass. "This just shows me that Dad doesn't think I can handle a position like that. Sorry, but I'm insulted."

She reached for a slice of bacon and placed it on her plate. "Have you talked to Dad about your feelings?"

Kellen shook his head. "No. There's no point, Zaire. He's already made up his mind."

She gave him a sympathetic look. "I'm sorry."

He shrugged in nonchalance, then busied himself fixing a plate of food.

Zaire stated, "I'm glad you're here because I'd like to talk to you about Dreyden." She wiped her mouth with a napkin again. "I think there's something going on with our brother."

"I feel the same way," Kellen responded. "I'm worried about him."

"He's losing so much weight, and he doesn't seem to eat as much as he normally does. That's totally not like Dreyden. That man loves to eat."

"Did you say anything to him?"

Zaire nodded. "He just brushed me off by saying that he's fine."

"He did the same to me," Kellen stated.

"I'm going to talk to Mama." She finished off her bacon. "Maybe she can find out what's wrong with him."

"She may already know but just doesn't want to betray Dreyden's confidence."

"You're right, but I'm still going to say something to her." Zaire took a sip of her juice. "How do you like the job so far?"

"It's okay. I've just been doing some shadowing," Kellen responded. He sampled the scrambled eggs.

"You don't sound excited at all."

"I'm not," he replied truthfully. "You wouldn't be excited either if you had to watch others doing what you want to do."

"Kellen, I better not hear you complaining of having too much work or feeling overwhelmed in a few months, because I'm going to remind you of this conversation."

"I won't, Zaire. I have a job and I'm grateful, but I would like to at least do what I've been hired to do."

"You need to learn patience."

"I am," he countered. "That's why I took the job."

"Kellen, I have to be honest with you. Your attitude really sucks," Zaire stated. "I certainly hope you're not going into the office like this."

He considered her words. "You're right. I'm going about this the wrong way."

"It's okay to be disappointed, but you can't let those feelings take over."

Kellen nodded in agreement. "I hear what you're saying."

"So what are you getting Harold and Amy for a wedding gift?" she asked.

He shrugged in nonchalance. "I don't know. I haven't even looked at the registry. I'll probably just give them a gift card. What are you getting them?" Kellen finished off his toast.

"I am struggling with that, actually. The man is rich and has everything. I don't have a clue what to get them."

"Maybe we should ask Livi for some suggestions. I'm sure she's come across some trinkets during her last buying trip."

"Kellen, that's a great idea. I'll give her a call this morning."

He finished off his breakfast, and then pushed away from the table. "I guess I'd better head to work."

"Try and have a good day."

"I'll give it a shot." Kellen broke into a grin. "You have a good one, too."

Ten minutes later, he was in the car and driving into Los Angeles. He had a couple of technical training classes on his agenda for today. Kellen didn't mind the training sequence; he enjoyed it. However, it was his appetite, making him hungry to get started on a project.

Might as well get this out of my mind, he thought. Addison was not going to allow him to work on anything until after he completed his training sequence.

She'd announced that she would not be in the office today until after lunch because she had a couple of off-site meetings. Kellen felt a thread of disappointment. He appreciated beauty and she was one stunning woman.

Addison was all business, though. Normally, he knew within minutes if he'd made a connection with a woman. Kellen could tell when a woman was attracted to him, but with his boss—he couldn't get a good read on her.

Not that he was looking to have a relationship with her. Kellen didn't really want to deal with problems on the job that a liaison could bring.

Chapter 3

By the time Saturday arrived, Kellen was more than ready to enjoy the weekend after a week of training classes and observing his coworkers as they worked on various projects.

Harold and Amy's wedding would be a great distraction.

A few years ago his family had been an embarrassment to their DePaul relatives, but they had finally managed to come together. Kellen was grateful. His father had often told them that they were stronger as a family. He agreed.

As a team, Malcolm and Harold were a force to be reckoned with. Harold had great ideas and vision for the future. It was Harold's idea to expand the Alexander-DePaul brand into other countries.

He gazed at the two-story, Cape Cod-style venue overlooking the ocean with an architect's eye. Harold and Amy had chosen the Swan Manor in Manhattan Beach for their wedding. It was the perfect choice for them, Kellen decided after overhearing his mother say the couple favored beautiful gardens and the beach.

He followed the stream of guests to the back of the house where cocktails were being served by a waitstaff dressed in black pants and bow ties with crisp, white shirts, amid bougainvillea, koi ponds and lush greenery. Kellen glimpsed the Pacific Ocean in the backdrop of the garden.

"This is very nice," Kellen heard Zaire remark. She and her husband arrived within seconds of him and Dreyden.

"Leave it to Harold to invite any and everyone on L.A.'s social register." He took a sip of his wine.

Dreyden chuckled. "Looks like he invited all of Hollywood, as well."

Kellen agreed. "The big jewels are definitely out of the safe today, and there is more couture out here than on the entire third floor of Neiman Marcus."

When time drew near for the ceremony to start, Kellen and his family made their way inside one of the elegant banquet rooms that was filled with light from French windows.

His mother dazzled in a royal purple Oscar de la Renta gown. Sage mingled nearby in a black-and-white Ralph Rucci haute couture gown from Paris while Zaire wore a turquoise-colored gown designed by Vera Wang with Cartier turquoise-and-diamond jewels.

Livi was the matron of honor. She walked up, looking lovely in a champagne gown with a train. "Has Blaze arrived?"

"I haven't seen him," Kellen responded.

"He should be here by now."

"Did you try to call him?"

She nodded. "It's going to voice mail."

He could see that she was worried, so Kellen told her,

"You go back and tend to the bride, Livi. I'll hunt down your husband."

Her lips turned upward. "Thanks."

Blaze arrived ten minutes later. "I heard there's supposed to be around seven hundred people at the wedding."

"Your wife was looking for you," Kellen stated. "You should call her."

He looked concerned. "Was she upset?"

Kellen laughed. "No...just worried."

"I left my phone at home," Blaze explained.

Kellen pulled out his phone. "Call Livi and let her know that you're here. She's dealing with enough, I would imagine, as the matron of honor."

Blaze agreed.

"Hey, baby, I'm here. I left my phone at the house by accident."

Kellen walked away to give Blaze some privacy as he talked to his wife. Mostly all of his siblings had found love, and he was happy for them. At this point in his life, he was not looking for a serious relationship. He wanted to focus on his career.

Inside the lavish mansion, Kellen noted that three large banquet rooms were converted into three distinct and equally chic rooms: one resembled a Parisian backdrop for the ceremony, another served as a luxury lounge and the third was the massive grand ballroom where the reception would be held. Golden lovebirds were situated among thousands of votive candles throughout.

Kellen sat down beside Dreyden, pulling at his bow tie. "I can't wait to get out of this tuxedo."

"I know what you mean."

Guests were seated while being entertained by a harpist.

Kellen and Dreyden were joined by the rest of their

family and DePaul relatives, taking up the first five rows on the groom's side.

Near boredom, he released a soft sigh when the processional began.

Twelve bridesmaids. Kellen hoped whoever he married didn't want a high-society wedding. He preferred something short and simple. He never understood why people wanted to spend so much money on a ceremony that lasted thirty to forty-five minutes at most.

Once the bride made a dramatic entrance, the ceremony didn't take long, much to Kellen's relief.

In the ballroom, after the pastor gave the blessing, more than a hundred perfectly choreographed attendants served dinner. After the bride and groom finished eating, they navigated around the room, pausing at each table to greet their guests.

When they reached Kellen and Dreyden, both men stood up.

"Congratulations, Mr. and Mrs. DePaul," Kellen stated as he gave Amy a hug.

"Thank you," they said in unison.

Dreyden embraced her and said, "Keep this man in line."

"Don't worry, she does," Harold responded with a big grin. "I'm glad you all could be here to share this day with us."

"I wouldn't have missed it."

Dreyden nodded in agreement.

The happy couple moved on to Zaire and Tyrese, who were seated at the same table along with Sage and Ryan.

"They really look good together," Kellen said in a low voice. "I don't think I've ever seen Harold so happy."

"She's good for him," Dreyden responded.

Harold's sister, Meredith, walked over with her husband. "Hello, cousins." Kellen hadn't had a chance to speak with her until now because she was also a brides-maid in the wedding.

He broke into a smile. "Marriage looks good on you both. I'm sorry I couldn't be here for your wedding."

"You were in the middle of your exams. We under-stood," Meredith told him. "Thank you for the beautiful gift you sent."

They talked a few minutes more before joining his siblings at the table. Dreyden and Kellen walked over to the bar to get something to drink.

"You know the pressure is about to increase for you to find a wife," Kellen told his brother.

Dreyden laughed. "What about you? You're single."

"I'm just starting out in my career, though. You have your own business and your own place. Sorry, but the focus is going to be on you, bro."

"I'm not seeing anyone seriously, so it might be a while."

Kellen laughed. "Mom's going to be so disappointed."

His brother chuckled.

The band, La Chapelle Rhénane Orchestra from Paris, kept the dance floor packed all night long.

Kellen finished the last of his champagne. "You know…I don't think I've ever seen Harold dance."

Dreyden glanced over at his brother and said, "It's his wedding day. He's having a good time."

"So what's going on with your love life?" he asked Dreyden. "I can't believe you haven't met anyone special."

"I've been so inundated with work that I haven't had time to build a relationship. However, there is this girl that I think is special. She's a workaholic just like I am. Only she's in Hong Kong. Her job transferred her there eight months ago."

"Bro, you need some downtime."

"I know. I am going to take some time off in a couple of months. I'm thinking about going to Hong Kong."

"I think you should, especially if she's special to you," Kellen advised.

"If I do that, I'm not sure I'll have a restful vacation."

He laughed. "I guess you're right about that."

"What about you?" Dreyden inquired. "Have you left anyone special behind in Atlanta?"

Kellen shook his head. "I'm not looking to get serious with anybody. I want to get my career on track first."

He accepted a second glass of champagne from a passing waiter. "There is a sea of gorgeous women here," he said. "It's been a while since I've seen so many in one place like this."

Dreyden agreed.

They stopped to chat with a couple of friends who were in attendance. Kellen smiled at the daughter of the couple he was conversing with. She smiled back and gave a little wave, but it was Dreyden who seemed to have captured her attention.

When they walked away, he said, "She was pretty. I saw the way she kept looking at you."

Dreyden chuckled. "Maybe I should ask her to dance."

"I think you should," Kellen encouraged. "Go on... have fun."

He watched his brother make his way back over to the young woman. They made their way to the dance floor.

"What's this?" Blaze asked as he joined Kellen at his table. "I guess Dreyden's feeling much better. He's out there dancing."

"He needs to have some fun. The man does nothing but work."

"What about you? When was the last time you had a date?"

"It's been a while," Kellen responded. "I didn't want

to be tied to anyone since I was moving out here right after graduation."

"So you're ready to break some hearts in Los Angeles."

He grinned. "I'm definitely not going to get mine broken."

"I can't wait to meet the woman who steals your heart, Kellen."

"Hey, I can't, either. She's really going to have to be something special to get me to want to settle down."

Kellen drove to Dreyden's condo the next day. He was looking forward to watching a basketball game with him. He was a Lakers fan while his brother favored the Atlanta Hawks.

"Hey, I just got off the phone with Ari," Dreyden announced. "He's bringing pizza and beer."

"Great," Kellen replied. He took note of Dreyden's grayish pallor and the dark circles beneath his eyes and the way his clothes hung loosely on his frame. "Hey, when was the last time you saw a doctor?" he inquired.

"I think it's been about two years," Dreyden responded with a slight shrug. "I think I may have a virus or something, but I don't think it's anything serious."

"I don't agree," Kellen responded. "This has been going on for a while now. I'm not the only one who has noticed how much weight you've lost, and that you haven't had much of an appetite lately."

"The whole family has said something." Dreyden was quiet for a moment. "If it's that noticeable, then I guess it's time for a checkup, at least."

"Make the call to the doctor's office."

"Enough about me," Dreyden said as he settled back in his chair. "Let's talk about you. How was your first week on the job?"

Kellen shrugged in nonchalance. "It was okay. I spent

most of the day in technical workshops and the rest getting familiar with some of our current projects. I haven't been able to touch anything yet."

"So what do you think of the new Special Projects Director?"

"When did you find out that Addison was getting the position?" Kellen asked.

"I think Ari may have mentioned it a couple of weeks ago."

"Why didn't you tell me?"

"Dad didn't want us to say anything," Dreyden responded. "He wanted to be the one to discuss it with you."

Kellen gave a short laugh. "There was no discussion. Dad straight out told me that he had given the job away. He didn't think that I could handle the position."

Dreyden took a long drink of his bottled water. "You're still upset with him, I see."

Shrugging in nonchalance, Kellen responded, "I don't agree with his decision, and I never will."

"Dad wasn't trying to hurt you."

"That may not have been his intention, but he did," he stated. "He clearly has no faith in my abilities."

"You're taking this the wrong way."

"I don't know any other way to take it, Dreyden. Dad didn't even consider giving me a chance to prove myself. He just gave the position to someone else."

"Kellen, do you honestly think that you could have gone to another company and walked into a director position with no experience?"

"I'm really tired of hearing that. Maybe I should put some feelers out there and see," he countered.

Dreyden scratched his arm before folding them both across his chest. "Maybe you should. Who knows…it may work out for you."

Kellen eyed his brother for a brief moment, noting the way he was scratching his skin.

"Dad would probably see it as a betrayal of some sort."

"No, I'm pretty sure he would understand," Dreyden uttered. "Dad has always allowed us to make our own choices. You're free to do whatever you want."

"I don't know what to do," Kellen said with a sigh of frustration.

"I would give the job six months," Dreyden stated. "If you still feel the same way, then start sending out your résumé."

He nodded in approval. "I can do that."

"I think I need to change the soap I'm using or something. My skin is dry and itchy."

Kellen chuckled. "I've told you about buying that cheap stuff. You need to stop being so frugal."

"And you need to start putting away some money for the future," Dreyden advised. "God bless the child that's got his own."

"You don't have to worry about me, big brother. You, Blaze and Ari have been good role models for me. I've learned from all of your mistakes."

"But have you learned from your own?"

Kellen laughed. "The jury's still out on that."

"Charles will provide leadership for all team members throughout the life of this project to ensure continuity, meaningful collaboration and clear communication," Addison stated Monday afternoon. "Kellen, I would like for you to shadow the team."

He gave a slight nod, but did not respond otherwise.

Kellen had been with the company for almost three weeks now and hadn't been able to touch a project. She could tell that he wasn't happy with her decision, but this project was too important to the company—Addison was not willing to risk placing a novice on something like this.

After the other employees left the room, she said, "I get the feeling that you're upset about my decision to just let you shadow the team."

"I'm here to work. All I've been doing since training ended is shadowing this person and that person."

"I understand that you're ready to jump in and get to work, however, you need to observe a few projects first."

"You saw my portfolio," Kellen uttered with a hint of arrogance. "You know what I can do. Is all this necessary? Why can't I learn by actually working on something?"

"This is a major project…"

"Oh, I get it," he responded. "You're afraid I'll make a mistake and it'll reflect badly on you. This is about you."

She responded coolly, "This isn't about me at all."

"You don't have to worry about me tarnishing your sterling reputation, Addison. I'll shadow the team as you decided, but I'm not about to let you think I'm okay with it."

Addison sat there, her cheeks on fire but trying desperately to appear calm, refusing to let Kellen see just how upset she was. "Kellen, I shadowed for a month before I was given a small project to work on. Just be patient."

"I hope you don't plan on having me shadow for a month."

She folded her arms across her chest. "Actually, I was thinking it might be a good idea."

"You can't be serious."

Addison met his gaze. "I am very serious about this, Kellen. Let me be clear. I'm not going to let you touch anything until I know that you're ready."

"I hear you, boss," he uttered before walking away.

She could not believe his gall. If she'd been a man,

there was no way that Kellen would talk to her this way. Clearly, he didn't like having a female in charge. Some men believed that female managers were emotional and leadership-ability lacking. She knew that some of her male employees felt that way. Well, she wasn't going anywhere. Addison led her teams with a firm hand, while being open to their thoughts and opinions.

In a way, Addison understood Kellen's desire to get to work. She had been the same when she started, but not as arrogant. He had a lot to learn about the specific technical parts of the job—things he wouldn't have learned in school. Kellen was very talented and he was intelligent. Still, there was so much he had to learn about his job.

Kellen sighed in frustration as he made his way home. Addison was just as bad as his father. Apparently, neither one of them had any faith in his skills. He'd spent the rest of his day at the office sitting in a conference room listening as a team of engineers discussed a project he wanted in on. It had been a struggle for him to just sit there quietly and contribute nothing.

At home, Kellen changed into a pair of sweats and a T-shirt. He needed to work out some of his aggravation.

"I suppose you're still angry with me," Malcolm said when he entered the exercise room.

Kellen shook his head. "I'm not angry, Dad. I'm just really disappointed with the way things turned out."

"I understand that. Do you want to talk about it?"

"It won't change anything," he responded. "So there's really nothing for us to discuss."

"Your mother made roast chicken for dinner," Malcolm announced. "Will you be joining us?"

"I'm going to have dinner out, but I won't be out late," Kellen answered. "I'm in the mood for Italian."

Malcolm stood in his path. "Son, I don't like this distance between us. I'm sorry that you're so disappointed and upset. It's not what I wanted for you."

"How did you expect me to feel, Dad?" he questioned, meeting his gaze.

"I knew that you would be disappointed, Kellen. It just didn't occur to me just how much you wanted the position, but even if it had—I stand by my decision."

"Dad, I accepted the position offered to me and I'm grateful to have a job, period. I know that you believe this is the best career path for me, but I don't agree."

"You're right. I do believe this is the best career path for you," Malcolm responded. "In time, you will feel the same way."

Kellen smiled. "We'll see, Dad."

"Why don't you stay and have dinner with us? Your mother would love to spend some time with you."

"What about you?"

"I would like that, as well."

"I'd like that, too," Kellen confessed. He was tired of being angry and he hated the distance between them. It was time to accept what he could not change and just move on.

Chapter 4

Kellen shifted in his seat to keep from falling asleep. The person he was shadowing talked in a monotone voice, which was boring him senseless. He rose to his feet. "I'll be right back."

He made his way to the break room. Hopefully, moving around a bit could wake him up some. It was nearly the end of August, and he was still taking workshops, working on mock projects and shadowing others. He was ready and anxious to work on real projects.

"Kellen?"

He turned around to find Addison standing in the doorway.

"Taking a break?" she inquired.

"Yes, I needed one." Despite his frustration with her, Kellen felt an invisible thread pulling them together. When he looked in her dark brown eyes and downward to her perfectly shaped lips, he felt the urge to taste them.

"Are you okay?" she inquired.

Kellen nodded. "I just came in here to get some water, but I'm glad you're here. Addison, I was thinking about something while observing Josie. That new civic center is a gem of a project. What it needs is a high-profile, progressive design that will enhance its reputation, such as building it on the waterfront."

"That was the original idea, but it means pier drilling and extensive foundation work. ADDG would have to foot the bills for this until the first payment comes in after the end of stage one. This job's too big for us, Kellen."

"Addison, you're thinking too small."

"I'm thinking within our means," she countered. "Thanks to your father, this company has never experienced any cash-flow problems. I definitely don't intend to accrue any on my watch."

"We're on solid financial footing, which means we could expand. If the city wants the center on the beach, then we should give them what they want," Kellen argued.

"We would need at least fifteen million dollars in reserve in order to do that. Don't get me wrong, it's a good idea," she said, "but it wouldn't be feasible for several reasons. One being that it would be much too expensive, and another is that your father would never give us his approval."

"I could talk to him," Kellen offered.

Addison shook her head. "I'm saying no to the idea." Her tone was firm and final.

Irked, he stalked out of the break room, heading back to observe his coworker.

She is going to be a problem, Kellen decided. He didn't fully understand why his father had so much faith in her. Surely, he wasn't swayed by her beauty.

A thread of shame snaked down his spine. He knew his father would never hire someone who was unquali-

fied. Even so, he included Kellen in the group of unquali-
fied individuals.

He had accepted his fate, but now he had to deal with
Addison. He couldn't help but wonder if she felt threatened by him.

After all, he was an Alexander.

Addison was still heavy on Kellen's mind by the time
he made it home. He put forth a valiant effort to put her
out of his thoughts, but it proved harder than he thought.

After work, Addison met Tia at the La Serenata de
Garibaldi located on East First Street for dinner.

"I love this place," she said, sliding into a booth near
the window. "It's one of my favorite restaurants."

"The food here is great," Tia responded. "Especially
the *Callos de Hacha a la Plancha*."

The grilled scallops topped with mushrooms, peppers
and onions were a good choice for appetizer. "I think I'll
have that, too, for starters. For my main entrée, I'll get the
fish enchiladas in green chile sauce," Addison stated with
a smile. "This is the perfect way to end a busy workday."

"Hey, isn't that your handsome employee over there?"

Addison stole a peek over her shoulder.

"Yeah," she responded as casually as she could manage, turning back to face her friend. "That's Kellen." He
was the last person Addison had expected to run into
here of all places. The thought that he had followed her
entered her mind, but she quickly chased it away. Why
would he do something like that?

"Did you mention that you were coming here for dinner?" Tia asked.

Addison shook her head. She realized her friend had
the same idea. "I'm sure this is a coincidence."

"I recognized him from the magazine articles and pictures on the internet about his family. He looks much better in person."

"If you like that sort, I guess," Addison uttered with a shrug of nonchalance. "I personally don't care for his arrogance."

Tia gave a short laugh. "I'm sure you can handle him."

"For sure," Addison responded with a chuckle.

"So what's he like?" Tia asked in a whisper that somehow managed to carry over the noisy din of the crowded dining hall.

"I have to be honest. Kellen can be so frustrating at times. He thinks that he can do whatever he wants because his last name is Alexander."

"I take it that you two are not getting along?"

"We don't get along at all," Addison uttered. "He doesn't respect me, Tia. If I say blue—he wants to make it red."

Tia frowned. "You just need to set him straight with a quickness."

Addison nodded in agreement. "You're right. I do need to have a conversation with him. As much as I don't want to fire my employer's son, it might just come to that."

"Maybe it's what he needs. You can't let Kellen Alexander run over you. Make sure he knows that you're the boss."

"He's so talented and smart, Tia. In fact, I'm pretty sure that he wanted my position but didn't get it, and this is why he has such an attitude."

"Well, it's good to see that his family doesn't hand out titles to the children just because they have Alexander as their last name."

Addison agreed. "Malcolm has always been fair. He's a lot like Robert DePaul."

Her gaze landed on Kellen.

When he laid eyes on her, Addison waved in greeting. He walked toward their table.

"Good evening, ladies," Kellen greeted.

"Hello," they said in unison.

Addison gestured toward her friend and announced, "This is Tia."

His full mouth moved slowly and she saw his white, perfectly straight teeth. But more than that, his face lightened as his smile reached right to his eyes and claimed Addison's ability to breathe in the process.

"Tia, it's nice to meet you." Kellen turned his attention back to Addison. "I see we have something in common."

"Imagine that," she murmured with a smile. "Are you having dinner alone?"

"Actually, I'm waiting on a friend." He glanced over his shoulder and said, "Here she comes now."

Her heart stuttered a bit, but Addison kept her expression blank.

A surprising surge of envy swept through her. She didn't know why it bothered her. A man who looked like him probably could have any woman he chose. She was pretty certain that he had a girlfriend somewhere in the world. Kellen was much too handsome to be single.

He made the introductions. "This is Carolyn. She and I attended grad school together."

"She's cute," Tia said when Kellen and Carolyn navigated to their table. "Do you think they're dating?"

"I don't know," Addison responded. "He introduced her as his friend. Maybe that's all they are."

"I don't know. They seem pretty cozy."

She glanced over her shoulder. Her gaze collided with Kellen's brilliant gray eyes and held. Addison felt a threat of embarrassment that he'd caught her staring.

Tia chuckled.

Addison turned her attention back to her best friend. "What's so funny?"

"You are. I know that you're attracted to Kellen Alexander."

"He's good-looking and I'm not blind, but being attracted to him—I'm not."

"This is me you're talking to, Addison."

"Okay, so I'm attracted to him, but he is my employee. I'm not going to cross that line."

Addison meant everything she was saying. It just wasn't as easy as that. She was acutely conscious of him sitting at the table behind her. His presence was strong—too strong for her to ignore.

It was after 11:00 p.m., and Kellen decided that he needed to find something to snack on—he could no longer ignore his grumbling stomach. He heated up a piece of grilled chicken that was leftover from his dinner earlier.

He could not stop thinking about Addison. The image of the woman floated to the forefront of his mind. He hadn't expected to run into her at the restaurant.

A smile formed as he recalled the look she had given Carolyn. It was as if she was jealous. The thought amused him. Kellen wondered if she had a boyfriend. Although frustrating at times, Addison was beautiful and smart. But she seemed guarded, as well, prompting him to wonder at the reason.

In the office, she was the ultimate professional. At times, he wondered if Addison ever let her hair down to have a good time. He observed her as she enjoyed dinner with her friend and noted that she still seemed a bit reserved.

He finished his meal and then headed upstairs to shower and change into a pair of sweats and a T-shirt.

Afterward, he settled down in the living room to watch television, although his mind was elsewhere. Kellen could not get Addison out of his mind. He was attracted to her, despite his efforts to resist that particular emotion.

The next morning, Kellen strolled into the kitchen. "Good morning."

"Good morning," his parents responded in unison.

"Did I interrupt something?" he inquired as he loaded his plate with homemade biscuits, bacon, scrambled eggs and grits. "Sounds like you two were in a deep conversation when I came in."

Barbara wiped her mouth with the edge of her napkin. "We were discussing the plans for a hotel in North Carolina."

"I'm assuming ADDG is handling all phases of the designs," Kellen said. He stuck a forkful of eggs in his mouth.

"They are," Malcolm confirmed. "Your mom suggested that we consider Atlanta, as well."

"I think that's a great idea, but have you thought about going international?"

Malcolm met his gaze. "You really think so, son?"

Kellen nodded. "I do."

He finished his breakfast while they continued to discuss the future of the company.

Fifteen minutes later, Kellen was in his car and on the freeway heading to the office in Beverly Hills. He could hardly wait to see Addison—he wanted to discuss his participation on the Alexander-DePaul Hotel project.

He sat his backpack in his office before heading to Addison's office.

"Can I talk to you for a minute?" Kellen asked from the doorway.

"Sure," Addison responded calmly. "Come in and have a seat."

Even now she was trying to assume control, he thought

silently. This was a woman who felt her position was threatened, and was determined to stand her ground.

"My dad mentioned that we are going forward with a new hotel in North Carolina."

"We are," she confirmed.

"I actually designed one while I was in school."

"The one in your portfolio?"

"Yes."

Addison sat up straight in her chair. "It's nice, but the design specifics are not what your father wants. It's too modern."

"I don't mind making changes," Kellen stated. "I can sit down with him and—"

"Your father has already approved the initial design of the hotel," Addison interjected.

His mouth tightened.

"Kellen, I know that you think you're ready to take on a project this size, but you still have so much to learn." Nervously, she moistened her dry lips. "It's a bit more involved."

"What is with you?" he asked.

"Excuse me?"

"Are you this threatened by me?" Kellen knew he was going too far, but he forged ahead.

Anger flashed in her eyes. "Just because you are an Alexander doesn't bother me in the least. I have been in your shoes, Kellen, and I had to learn the technical. You have to do the same thing."

"I studied hotel models in college, Addison. I do know what I'm doing. Besides that, I *am* an Alexander." He studied her face for a moment to see if her expression would change, but it remained the same.

After a moment she got up and closed the door to her office. "It's becoming pretty obvious that we can't work together."

"So what are you saying?" he wanted to know, folding his arms across his chest.

"I'm saying that you're fired, Kellen."

His eyebrows rose in surprise. "I'm sure I didn't hear you correctly."

"You're fired," Addison repeated. "I have treated you fairly and as any other associate, but you insist on challenging me at every turn. I can't have you here undermining me or my leadership."

He met her gaze straight on. "You can't fire me."

"I just did."

"You're making a huge mistake, Addison. My father is not going to let this stand."

"At some point, you need to take responsibility for your choices in life and stop counting on your father to bail you out."

Anger flooded through him. "I don't need my dad to bail me out of anything. You have an issue with men. You're so insecure in your position that you don't know how to just be a leader. In fact, I think my being an Alexander *does* bother you, Addison. I have the talent and the brains for this. I know it and you know it, too."

"You have a lot of potential, Kellen," she admitted. "You also have a lot of arrogance, which overshadows that potential. You're a brilliant man, but your egotism gets in the way. It's such a waste of talent."

"This isn't over," he uttered before storming out of her office. Kellen shook with anger. He imagined that Addison would have a hard time explaining to Malcolm that she had just fired his son.

Chapter 5

Wet, yellow leaves clung to the rain-slicked, winding road. Kellen handled the curves in the path with confidence, his Audi A6 hugging the pavement. He switched on his headlights, drumming his fingers on the steering wheel in rhythm to the old-school music blasting from his Bose speakers. But no matter how fast Kellen drove, he couldn't outrun his fury.

His tires squealed as they spun slightly, seeking a connection with the rural highway.

Twenty minutes later, he walked into the house and tossed his keys on the table in the foyer. Kellen heard the television in the family room and headed in that direction.

I might as well get this over with.

His mother was sitting on the love seat, completely engrossed in the book she was reading.

"Hey, Mom," he greeted, grinding his teeth in frustration.

"What are you doing home so early?"

"I got fired," Kellen announced.

"What on earth happened?"

"Dad hired the wrong person, but that's just my opinion," he uttered. "I wanted her to consider my design for the new hotel in North Carolina, but she wasn't interested. She said it wasn't what Dad wanted. I offered to make any necessary revisions."

"Did she give you the reason why?"

"She didn't give one and it wouldn't have mattered if she had. I was honest and I told her that I felt she was holding me back. I've gone through the technical training and passed everything. All she wants me to do is shadow—she won't even give me a small project to work on. She didn't like it and she fired me."

"Do you have the design with you?"

"Yes," Kellen responded as he opened his portfolio and laid it on the table.

"This is very nice." Barbara looked at him. "I don't suppose she told you that your father's vision for the North Carolina hotel is to re-create the old DePaul Hotel."

He was surprised. "No, she didn't tell me this."

Malcolm walked into the kitchen. "I just got off the phone with Addison. Kellen, what were you thinking?"

"So I guess you're going to let Addison fire me just like that?" Kellen asked. "Without even hearing my side of things."

Malcolm nodded. "Addison told me that you accused her of being threatened by your talent and your being an Alexander. If this is true, then you deserved it, son."

"I just want the chance to actually work on a project. That's what I'm there for, Dad," he argued. "And I do feel that Addison is threatened by me."

"Believe it or not, you do not know everything, Kellen. I need you to understand something. You have to learn how to be led before you can lead."

"You didn't even know your father and he left you a multimillion-dollar estate. He didn't even have a relationship with you—yet he entrusted all of this to you."

"This is not about trust."

"Dad, you and I are never going to agree on this subject. I'm sorry."

"Kellen, sometimes you just have to learn the hard way…so be it." Malcolm walked out of the kitchen.

He turned and looked at his mother.

Barbara didn't utter a word.

"I liked it much better when you and Dad were just my parents."

Kellen went to his room and packed a bag. He didn't want to stay in this house with his parents a moment longer. He called Dreyden and asked, "Can I crash at your place for a couple of days?"

"Sure."

"I'll be there shortly."

"What happened?" Dreyden questioned immediately after Kellen arrived. "What are you and Dad fighting about now?"

"Addison fired me," he announced as he settled down in the living room. The three-bedroom condo featured floor-to-ceiling windows similar to the ones in the Alexander-DePaul Hotel & Spa residences in Beverly Hills. Dreyden had chosen to buy a place elsewhere, instead of living at the hotel.

"Dad's not going to override her decision, right?"

Kellen nodded. "He's supposed to have my back."

"This does not mean that he doesn't," Dreyden countered. "Dad wants his children treated like any other employee. You know that."

"I need to start looking for another job, thanks to Addison Evans."

"What is your responsibility in this?" Dreyden asked. "You do have to take ownership for your part."

Kellen frowned as he met his brother's gaze. "What are you talking about? I just wanted to know why she wouldn't let me work on any projects. I wanted to know why she was trying to hold me back."

"You gave Addison a hard time, but do you really think that you're ready to take on a project? You just started working."

"How would I know if not given the chance?" Kellen asked.

"It's pretty obvious that you don't trust Addison. Why is that?"

"It's the other way around. She doesn't trust me, Dreyden."

"Okay, so you don't trust each other. I ask the same question: Why is that?"

Kellen shrugged in nonchalance. "I don't know what her problem is—I am just ready to get to work."

"Maybe she didn't think that you're ready, little brother. She comes with a lot of experience—you have to give her some credit, Kellen. And one thing you need to remember. You have to crawl before you can walk."

"I learn more by doing."

Dreyden settled back in his chair. "Did you tell her that?"

Kellen shook his head. "Not really."

"Perhaps the conversation should have started there," Dreyden advised.

"You have a point," he acknowledged. "I jumped straight to accusing her of holding me back intentionally."

"No wonder she fired you. I can't say that I would've reacted any differently in her shoes."

"Thanks."

"You know I'm going to be straight with you, and you didn't handle this the right way, Kellen."

"I'm beginning to see that," he admitted. Kellen had no idea how he was going to make things right with Addison. He had a feeling that it was much too late for that. He'd messed up big-time.

"You can't take things so personally," Dreyden was saying.

"I guess it doesn't matter now," Kellen stated. "I no longer have the job."

"Why are you giving up so easily? Talk to Addison and convince her to give you another chance."

Kellen could tell Dreyden was getting sleepy. He was yawning nonstop and his speech was a bit slurred. "Why don't you go on to bed? I don't need you to babysit me."

"I think I will," he responded. "I'll see you in the morning."

Kellen did not stay up too long after his brother went to bed. He watched the news and then headed to the spare bedroom.

The guest room was highlighted in a walnut-colored crown molding complementing the wine-and-gold color palette throughout. The small sitting room featured a sofa, TV and an overstuffed chair with floor lamps.

Kellen considered calling Addison but decided that not enough time had passed. She was probably still angry with him and wouldn't listen to anything he had to say. He thought it best to give it a few days.

He had made a complete fool of himself.

Kellen realized that he never should have come at Addison the way he did—it was not the most professional way to behave. He had let his ego overcome his senses.

What is wrong with me?

However, the more important question was how he was going to set things right between him and Addison.

* * *

I actually fired Kellen Alexander.

When she gave the news to Malcolm earlier, Addison could tell by his tone that he was not pleased; however, he told her that he would back her decision. She also made him aware that should Kellen prove he was ready to work under her leadership, he would be welcomed back.

Only thing, though, Addison was relieved that Kellen was gone. At least now he wouldn't be such a distraction for her. It was a selfish thought and she knew it, but it didn't change how she felt. A thread of guilt snaked down her spine. Perhaps she had been rash in her decision to fire him.

Addison tossed the thought out of her mind. She would never behave so unprofessionally. She needed to teach Kellen a lesson, however. He would have to respect her as his boss.

Addison hadn't really wanted to fire him like that, but he had given her no other choice. She preferred to have him as an ally and not an enemy.

When she gave him the news, there wasn't a flicker of emotion in Kellen's expression, and the muscles in his face were rigid. Although he tried not to show it, he was understandably upset.

She was going to miss seeing his handsome face at the office, and that sexy grin of his. It was hard not to respond to the open friendliness in Kellen's face, the amusing curiosity in his eyes. He had tried to challenge her a few times. However, she could not let Kellen disrespect her. It did not matter that he was an Alexander—at least not to her. She intended to treat him the same as the other members of her team.

Addison picked up a ruler to measure the dimensions of a project she was reviewing.

Yeah, things definitely weren't going to be the same now that Kellen was gone. She felt a profound sadness deep within.

Saturday morning, Kellen woke up early to work out.

Afterward, he showered and changed into a pair of sweats and a T-shirt, and then made his way to the kitchen to help his mother prepare for a family cookout.

"I guess I need to find a place of my own," he announced. "I'm sure you and Dad are enjoying being empty-nesters."

Barbara laughed. "Honey, we enjoy having you home with us. It's been a long time." She retrieved a covered pan laden with raw fish from the refrigerator and sat it down on the counter.

"Still, it's time for me to get a place of my own."

"If that's what you want, Kellen," she responded. "We're not rushing you out of the house. Have you met someone special? Is that why you're in such a hurry to move?"

"No, Mom…this has nothing to do with a woman." He picked up a can of beans. "I'll make the baked beans," Kellen announced, changing the subject. He didn't want to get his mother started on his love life.

Barbara did not press him. She seemed caught up in her preparation of the food, seasoning the meat for the grill. "Thanks, sweetie."

He sat a large pot on the stove.

"Have you decided what you're going to do about your job?" Barbara asked.

"What can I do?" Kellen countered while pouring the beans into the pot. "I was fired."

"Why don't you go talk to Addison," his mother suggested. "Maybe you can try and work things out."

"I don't think it would work."

Barbara glanced over her shoulder at him. "Now, I know you're not about to give up on something that you want. This is not my child talking like that."

Kellen chuckled. "Addison and I can't work together, Mom. I think that much is pretty obvious."

His mother turned around to face him. "Can you say that you've honestly tried working with her?"

He thought long and hard before he responded. "In all honesty—maybe not."

"Then why not try a different approach?" Barbara began making hamburger patties. "Talk to Addison and keep an open mind."

"I guess the worst thing she can say is that she's not going to give me my job back." Kellen added barbecue sauce, a family recipe, to the beans.

Barbara nodded. "It can't hurt."

Two hours later, Kellen sat outside on the patio with Ari and his family. Sage and Ryan arrived a few minutes later followed by Zaire and Tyrese.

Zaire moved about the kitchen, helping her mother apply the finishing touches to the meat. Malcolm carried it outside to the grill.

Kellen saw his nephew sitting by himself. He got up and walked over to the lounge chair. "What's up, Joshua?"

"Nothing," he responded.

"What's wrong?" Kellen asked, noting the unhappy look on his face.

"I want to play video games, but Mommy said I couldn't and I'm bored."

"Why don't we do something else?"

"Like what?"

Kellen tried to think of something to do with his nephew. Eleven-year-old Joshua was in remission from leukemia. Three years ago, he had to attend school via satellite because of low blood counts, which placed him at risk for infection. He was still being monitored by his doctors for side effects of the chemotherapy treatments he received.

"How about playing some basketball?"

"You're gonna play with me?" Joshua asked.

"Only if you promise not to beat me too badly."

"I promise." Joshua burst into laughter.

"I don't know," Kellen said. "I'm not convinced from the way you're laughing. You were killing them on the football field."

"Uncle Dreyden said he loved coaching me. He said that I listened and did what I was told."

"I know."

"This season I might get to play all four quarters," Joshua stated. "My doctors say that I'm doing real good. I still have to be real careful, though."

"That's great news," Kellen said.

"Where is Uncle Dreyden?" Joshua wanted to know.

Kellen was wondering the same thing. "He should be here shortly."

He and Joshua walked over to the basketball court.

Joshua scored six points courtesy of Kellen. He enjoyed seeing his nephew laughing and playing like any other normal boy. He was not the same little fragile child he'd met a few short years ago.

Dreyden arrived minutes before they settled down to eat.

"Hey, I called you twice to see if you were coming, but I didn't get an answer," Kellen told him. "I was getting worried."

"I'm fine," was Dreyden's response.

"Have you seen a doctor yet?"

"You don't have to keep asking me about this," he snapped in irritation. "I told you that I'm doing fine."

Kellen was taken aback by his brother's tone. This

wasn't like Dreyden at all. "Sorry for being concerned, man."

"I shouldn't have spoken to you like that. I'm sorry, Kellen."

"It's okay," he responded, not trying to pretend he wasn't affected.

Dreyden sat down beside his brother. "Kellen, I really didn't mean to be so snappish."

"We're just worried about you."

"I know, and I love you all for it, but I'm tired of everyone bugging me about seeing a doctor. I just had a bug."

Kellen wasn't convinced, but he didn't want to argue with Dreyden.

"Are you okay?" Sage inquired when she strolled into the house and found him alone in the family room. "You look upset."

"I'm fine," he huffed. "I just wish that Dreyden would see a doctor. He keeps saying that it's just a bug, but he hasn't gone to the doctor for a checkup."

"None of us likes going to the doctor," she pointed out. "When was the last time you had a checkup?"

"It's been a while," Kellen responded. "But there's nothing wrong with me. I'm healthy."

"Well, our brother is a grown man. We can't force him into anything. I guess we should just let him be."

"I guess," he murmured.

After everyone left the house, Kellen found his father in the library.

"Dad…I really want to get my job back. I'll do whatever it takes."

Malcolm folded his arms across his chest. "Are you sure about this, Kellen?"

Kellen nodded. "I want to make this work with ADDG. It means everything to me to be able to work in the family business. I realized that I went in acting entitled, and it was wrong."

"If you want your job back, then I think you should talk to Addison."

"I intend to go in Monday morning," Kellen stated. "I just hope I can get Addison to give me another chance."

He missed the warmth of Addison's smile and the cute little way she wrinkled her nose whenever she was focused on her work. Kellen was looking forward to getting back to the job. He had to convince Addison that he was ready to be a team player, and that he was an asset to the company.

Chapter 6

"What are you doing here?" Addison asked when she found Kellen waiting for her outside her office the following Monday.

"You can't bar me from the building. My father still owns this place."

"Okay, so why did you come to this department?" she demanded. Her words came out tight and breathless. "In case you've forgotten, you don't work here anymore."

Kellen wasn't imagining the determined tilt to her chin, or the barely veiled antagonism.

"Actually, that's why I'm here, Addison," he responded. "I want to apologize for my behavior." Kellen grinned. "I even bought you flowers."

His charm wasn't wasted on her.

"Thank you," Addison said clearly. "But I still don't quite understand why you're really here. It must be important since you felt the need to try and impress me with roses."

She sniffed the pink blossoms and admitted, "Even if they are quite stunning."

Addison met his gaze. "You'd better get to the point. I'm afraid the novelty of these will wear off quick."

"I'd like you to give me another chance."

She bit back a smile. "It's going to take more than a rose bouquet to convince me that you're ready to work in this unit. Kellen, you and I can't work together. You have a problem working under me."

"I've given you a hard time, and I was wrong for it."

"Tell me something…why do you want to come back to the team?" she asked. "Is this out of loyalty to your father or do you really want to be here?"

"It's both," Kellen stated. "I want to work with my family, and I enjoy the projects we produce. This is where I belong, Addison."

"I'm not going anywhere and I will not have you undermining or disrespecting me. I want to make that clear."

"Understood," he responded.

"Are you sure?"

Kellen nodded. "I give you my word…if you let me come back, you won't regret giving me a second chance."

Addison folded her arms across her chest. "Please see that I don't."

"Okay, boss lady." Kellen removed his backpack, asking, "What's on the agenda?"

Their gazes locked—hers wary and uncertain, his impossible to read.

She shrugged. "You can work with Charles and Andrew on the project for the Arizona property. Let's see how well you work with a team."

"Not a problem. I can be a team player." He grinned, a flash of white teeth making her knees embarrassingly weak.

But putting up with Kellen Alexander also meant ignoring the way her heart took off at a gallop when he was around. He seemed to fill any space he was in, changed the air pressure and the temperature. He made her body feel hypersensitive as if just his nearness was a caress across her bare skin.

Addison smoothed her hair with shaking hands. "Kellen, I'll check in with you in a bit. I have some work to do," she said.

She went about her routine on autopilot, desperately aware that Kellen was two doors down from her office.

She wasn't in love with Kellen Alexander—it was more like an intense fascination built on searing sexual attraction. Addison didn't want to admit that she ached for the man constantly.

She was not ready for this.

Not at all.

"I was wondering if you'd like to have dinner with me," Kellen inquired at the end of the workday. "It's my way of saying I'm truly sorry for the way I acted before."

"We're fine," she responded. "You don't have to take me out."

"It's not a date," he clarified. "Just dinner. You *have* to eat."

Addison considered his words. "Okay. Dinner is fine."

"Why don't we eat at the Premiere Italiante in Hollywood?" Kellen suggested. "My family owns the restaurant, but I've never eaten there."

"Sounds good," she said. "I've heard good things about it, but I haven't tried it, either. I'll drive my car and meet you there."

He was surprised. "Really?"

Addison nodded. "Yeah. I think we should take both cars."

He smiled. "You're still concerned about what others will think."

"I don't want anyone getting the wrong impression, Kellen."

"People are going to think whatever they want, Addison," he said. "You can't let others define who you are."

Low lamplight, fresh flowers in vases and plants littered every tabletop while mauve wallpaper was pasted to the walls. Kellen sat across the table from Addison, admiring her beauty.

"You do realize that you're staring at me," she said as she laid down her menu.

"I'm sorry. I didn't mean to stare, but I couldn't help myself. You're a beautiful woman."

She waved her hand in dismissal. "Let's not go there, Kellen."

"Hey, I was just giving you a compliment. I didn't mean any harm."

"None taken, but it's not necessary," she responded.

He laughed. "I'm not trying to seduce you, Addison."

She flushed in embarrassment. "I never said that you were."

He eyed her. "Then what's the problem?"

Kellen's wry humor kept Addison on the verge of laughter as they dined on filet mignon, baby asparagus and large, fluffy baked potatoes.

"Now you're the one staring," he said.

She seemed a little embarrassed to have gotten caught. "You're a little hard to read, Kellen."

He gave a slight shrug before shifting his position in the seat. "What you see is what you get when it comes to me."

She smiled. "I would say the same about me."

Kellen smiled. "I don't know. I would say that you're very guarded. I'd just like to know the reason why."

* * *

His response took her by surprise. "You think I have walls up?"

Kellen nodded. "I would like to get to know Addison Evans—the person. I have a one-dimensional view of who you are."

She understood what he was saying, but she did not want to risk getting too personal with her employees. Past experiences had taught her to be wary.

"I've been burned before," Addison stated. "Someone tried to sabotage me after I let them get too close. I won't let it happen again."

"I'm not that person and neither are your other employees. Do you believe that someone on your team wants your job?"

She met his gaze. "I thought you wanted it."

"I did," Kellen confessed. "But I wouldn't try to sabotage your work to get the job."

Addison took a sip of her water. "I have to admit that I thought you'd be given the job, anyway."

He laughed. "Then you don't know my dad very well."

"I admit I was wrong." Addison settled back in her chair. "However, I want you to know that I enjoy working with you. I've never encountered someone with so much natural talent and ability."

"I feel like I was born to do this," Kellen said. "It's my passion."

She nodded in understanding. "I've felt the same way since I was five years old. My mother loved looking at model homes. We would pretend that it was our home and we'd talk about the things we'd change. I would take floor plans and make additions...changes...stuff like that."

He smiled. "I used to buy home-design magazines and do the same thing. I could sit and draw for hours."

Kellen finished off his food. "I appreciate your sharing this with me."

"You're pretty easy to talk to," Addison responded.

"I'm glad you feel this way. I feel in order to click as a team, you have to take time to get to know one another."

She smiled. "Point taken."

Kellen broke into a grin. "Do you trust me?"

"Yeah, I do. Why?"

"Because I'm going to order dessert for us. It's my mother's favorite, and she raves about it."

Addison met his gaze. "I'll try almost anything once."

Kellen had a hard time admitting it, but Addison had a lot more experience and was very knowledgeable in their field of work. She tackled every project with heart and the longer he worked there, the more he came to admire her work ethic.

He glanced up from his computer monitor just as Harold walked into the office. "What are you doing here?"

"I was in the area and I figured I'd come see if you had some time for lunch."

"Sure." Kellen pushed away from his desk. He needed to take a break. He'd spent all morning glued to his computer. Addison had given him his first solo project and he wanted it to be perfect.

"Looks like you're working hard."

"I am," Kellen confirmed.

They walked across the street to a restaurant on the corner.

"So how is married life?"

Harold grinned. "I'm loving it. Amy is wonderful, and she makes me happy. To be honest, I'm crazy about her."

Kellen chuckled. "You sound just like Ari and Blaze when they got married. Do you really feel that way or is it something that you're supposed to say?"

"Wait until you find that special woman you want to marry," Harold responded. "You will be singing the same anthem."

"I'm not sure I'm marriage material. My career is definitely the priority in my life right now." As he said the words, an image of Addison floated across his mind.

Kellen had developed genuine feelings for her but had not acted on them. She was slowly letting her guard down around him and he didn't want to do anything to put the progress he'd made with her at risk.

"How is William doing?" he asked.

Harold gave a sad smile. "Not well at all. I don't think my brother is going to be around much longer."

"I'm sorry."

He shrugged. "Death is a part of life."

"It still hurts the same," Kellen responded.

"Meredith has been great with taking care of him. He has a private nurse, but my sister insists on being with William for every treatment. She was the same way with Uncle Robert."

"I heard the same thing about you, Harold. You never left his side, either."

He gave a tiny smile. "That's what you do for family."

"I agree completely," Kellen told him.

They finished their lunch and headed back to the office.

"When you have some free time on your hand, Amy and I would love to have you join us for dinner one evening."

"As long as you're not trying to hook me up."

Harold laughed. "I'll tell the wife."

Kellen headed to his office after saying goodbye to his cousin. He fought against all thoughts of Addison before they consumed his mind. The last thing he wanted was a serious relationship with any woman—yet he could not escape the hold that the gorgeous boss lady had on him.

Chapter 7

Kellen and his family were present for the grand opening of the Alexander-DePaul Center. He was surprised when he saw Addison enter through the double doors. She looked stunning in a navy dress and silver high-heeled sandals.

He met her halfway. "Addison, I didn't know you were coming."

"We worked very hard to bring your father's vision to life," she responded. "I wanted to be here when the doors opened."

Kellen was thrilled to see her, although he tried not to show it. He didn't want to spook her. "I hope you don't mind my saying that you look beautiful."

"Thank you. You don't look too bad yourself," Addison responded warmly.

He escorted her over to a table and pulled out the chair for her.

"Always the perfect gentleman," she murmured.

"My mama raised me right." Kellen sat down beside her.

Addison laughed.

Her laughter set his pulse fluttering. He ignored the sudden surge in his pulse and maintained an even tone. "Would you like something to drink?"

"A glass of white wine, please."

Kellen returned a few minutes later with her drink.

"Duty calls. I have to join my family for now, but I won't be gone long."

He walked briskly across the room where his family had gathered for media photos. Homelessness was a cause that Kellen and his family cared deeply about—it was one they were determined to do what they could to help those who found themselves in this situation.

"I see Addison's here," Dreyden whispered. "Did you invite her?"

"No," he whispered back. "Dad must have invited her."

"So what are you going to do about it?"

"Make the most of my time with her," Kellen responded with a grin.

"Would you like to dance?" he asked when he returned to the table.

"Sure."

Addison was a good dancer, he noted as he watched her body move to the rhythm of the music.

They danced to three songs before Kellen escorted her off the floor. "I really like this side of you."

She smiled up at him. "I do let my hair down every now and then."

"Glad to hear it," Kellen replied. "I wasn't sure if you knew how to have fun."

Addison paused in her steps. "Really?"

He nodded. "In the office you're always so focused on work."

"Like you, I take my job very seriously," she stated.

"I don't think there's any harm in having fun while you're on the job."

She gave him a sidelong glance. "Kellen, is this your way of saying that we don't have fun at work?"

He gave a short chuckle. "That's not what I'm saying at all. Why don't we change the subject before I get into trouble?"

Addison laughed. "I think that's a good idea."

Kellen's eyes traveled the room. "You all did a great job on this center," he said. "This is exactly what my father envisioned."

"This was actually a labor of love for me," Addison admitted. "Homelessness is a cause that I'm very passionate about. I volunteer at the L.A. Mission once a month."

Kellen wasn't surprised. He'd witnessed her buying lunch for a homeless man who hung out at the end of the block. He knew that she had a generous nature. "There was a young man in Atlanta, attending college and homeless. I invited him to stay in my apartment. I hated the thought of someone like him living on the streets. I bought him a laptop and promised him that he could stay in the apartment until he graduated."

"That's very generous of you, but how did he end up homeless?"

"His mother died and he couldn't pay rent. He was evicted from their apartment."

Kellen met her gaze. "He managed to keep his grades up during all of this. I felt he deserved a chance."

"I agree."

"Addison, what area do you live in?" Kellen asked. "I imagine you somewhere on the beach."

"I live on Figueroa at the Apex."

"Nice…" he murmured.

She met his gaze. "I bet you live in one of those luxury residences at the Alexander-DePaul Hotel."

Kellen shook his head. "Right now I'm living with my parents, but I've been looking for a place of my own."

"I'm sure you could have your pick at the hotel."

"I could, but I'm more like Dreyden and Blaze when it comes to living quarters. I want my own space away from the family."

"So where have you been looking?" Addison asked. She took a sip of her drink.

"West L.A., Beverly Hills… I really like the Century, though."

She agreed. "They are really nice. I looked at them but decided to go with the Apex, instead. They were a little too rich for my blood."

"What you pay in rent at the Apex, I'm sure you could afford the mortgage on a condo at the Century."

She laughed. "You're probably right."

"C'mon, let's dance," he said, rising to his feet. "I really like this song."

Addison allowed him to take her by the hand and lead her to the crowded dance floor.

"Hey, I have a couple of football tickets for the 49ers game on Sunday," Kellen announced when the song ended and they were on the way back to their table. "If you're interested, we can fly up to San Francisco on my father's jet Saturday evening or early Sunday morning. We'd have a good time."

"You really can't think it's a good idea for us to hang out together," Addison responded.

He was surprised by her statement. "Why not? We both love football."

She gave a slight shrug. "I don't know, Kellen. I just don't think it's a good idea."

"I don't agree," he responded. "It's the perfect opportunity to get to know one another."

Addison gave him a sidelong glance. "And why would I want to get to know you better?"

"Because you're curious," Kellen responded with a grin. "You would never admit it, but I'm pretty sure that you are interested in me."

"I'm interested in all of my employees."

He smiled. "If you go to the game with me, you'll get to see a different side of my personality."

"That's what I'm afraid of," Addison responded with a wry smile. "Enjoy your game."

"You're going to miss out on a great game."

"I'm sure."

Kellen accepted two glasses of white wine from the tray of a passing waiter. He gave one to Addison and kept the other for himself. He sat down beside her.

"This is a really nice event."

"My mother and sisters worked together to pull this off," he responded. "Zaire came up with the theme and they just ran with it."

"I love that you're so close to your family, and you're very proud of their accomplishments. I think that's nice."

"Do you have any siblings?" Kellen asked.

"No, I'm actually an only child—more like an orphan now since my mother passed away."

He glimpsed the sadness in her eyes, prompting him to ask, "How long has she been gone?"

"Two years."

"What about your father?"

"He died when I was twelve years old. Then it was just me and Mom." She smiled. "Let's talk about something happier."

The tiny peek at her tongue sent a shot of adrenaline through Kellen and the fine hairs on his body standing on end.

"C'mon and change your mind, Addison. We both

love the 49ers. Let's go to the game and cheer them on to victory."

She shot him a skeptical look.

Kellen held up both hands. "I promise that I'm not looking for anything more than someone to enjoy the game with."

"Why not take one of your brothers?" she questioned.

"Because none of them are huge fans of the 49ers, for one thing. I want to take someone who will actually enjoy the game."

Kellen strode into Addison's office and placed a ticket on her desk. "The ticket is yours. I hope to see you at the game."

He left her office before she could utter a response.

Addison loved football, and she especially wanted to see the 49ers play the New Orleans Saints, but she wasn't sure if it was a wise idea to attend a game with Kellen. She had even considered buying tickets but couldn't get good seats.

She picked up the one Kellen left and looked at it. *This is a really great seat.*

"I can't do this," Addison whispered. "He's my employee and it wouldn't look right."

She considered the art show she attended with Lisa, another member of the team who reported to her. Addison had also gone to another function with another employee. Maybe she was just overreacting.

Addison glanced down at the ticket. She really preferred to see the game live.

She couldn't believe that she was acting so foolish about this.

I'm a grown woman. I can go to a game with Kellen and not end up in bed with him. Besides, he's been nothing but a perfect gentleman.

Still, she decided to take some time to think about her decision.

On the following Saturday, Addison scrunched down in the driver's seat of her rental car and pulled her ball cap low over her eyes, hands clenched on the steering wheel. She was parked near the main gate of the Candlestick Park stadium.

Near the entrance stood Kellen Alexander, a man she was sure that she should avoid at all cost, but was powerless to do so. He looked even more handsome in his football jersey and cap. Her skin tingled.

Kellen was one of Beverly Hill's most eligible bachelors. He graduated from grad school with honors; he had brains, money, good looks and charm. Despite the fact that he could charm diamonds off a jewel thief with his generous smile and smooth manners, he projected an air of utter masculinity.

Really, who could resist him? she rationalized.

The truth was that Kellen was the real deal. She had a strong feeling that he was an amazing lover. Feeling her cheeks heat up, Addison moved restlessly, suddenly too hot in her team jersey and denim Capri pants.

"Is this seat taken?"

The moment Kellen heard her voice, his lips turned upward into a smile. He glanced up at Addison and smiled wider. "You're here."

She sank down into the empty seat beside him. "Yes, I decided I would rather watch the game live than on television."

"I really didn't think that you'd come, but I'm glad you're here." Even in a baseball cap and a football jersey, she looked stunning.

Addison smiled at him. "I just couldn't resist coming to cheer on my favorite team."

"Likewise," Kellen murmured.

She was like a kid at a candy store. He had never seen her so animated and filled with excitement. When the 49ers scored a touchdown, she jumped out of her seat, cheering.

"Now that's the way to start a game," she said.

Addison laughed with her head thrown back, and the sound of it hit Kellen right in the center of his chest. And when those sexy brown eyes blinked back at him, he felt the warm pull of attraction firing through his body nearly knock the reason right out of him.

He'd thought it couldn't get any better than the laugh. But then he'd heard the laugh coupled with the squeals of delight and gotten an eyeful of Addison's sensational and perfectly displayed backside as she shimmied in some victory after the second touchdown.

"Okay, guys," she yelled. "Third and six. Hold 'em."

Kellen eyed her in amusement. Addison was completely immersed in the game. He could have left and she wouldn't have noticed. Some of the women in his past pretended to like football but eventually revealed how much it bored them. Others displayed no love for the game at all. He found her a refreshing change.

"How do you know so much about football?" Kellen asked.

"Growing up, I used to watch my dad coach Pop Warner teams. I found the game fascinating and so I wanted to learn more. Both my parents were passionate about football. On Sundays after church you could find us in front of the television watching a game. I love the atmosphere of intensity and joy at a football game. I love the strategy of the game. I love how a well-formed team with a good battle plan can overcome a more powerful team."

"I totally get what you're saying. I admire those guys and at times, envy them—playing a game with heart and passion... I believe in doing something you love, and getting paid for it is a plus. It's the same way that I feel about what I do."

Addison nodded in understanding.

"Would you like to grab some dinner?" he inquired after the game ended.

"Sure."

As she walked, Kellen studied her backside, liking the set of her shoulders, the determined tilt of her head, the way her jeans fit her.

Addison slowed down a bit, allowing him to catch up with her. "Do you have a certain restaurant in mind?"

"No, do you?"

"Why don't we drive until we find one that looks inviting?" Kellen suggested.

"I'm feeling adventurous."

They decided on one that was about four blocks from the stadium.

Addison was mildly surprised by the soothing atmosphere of the restaurant. The mural of New Orleans and the smooth sounds of jazz playing in the background immediately put the diners in a relaxed mood, melting away the tensions of everyday life temporarily.

Her eyes traveled to Kellen.

"So what do you think?" he asked.

"This is nice," she said, her eyes bouncing around the restaurant that was draped in rich, but soothing jewel tones.

Waiters started to bring the food out, arranging it attractively on the table. They started with antipasto—asparagus spears wrapped in prosciutto and balsamic-glazed cipollines and sautéed beef tips.

As they dined, Addison acknowledged that Kellen had a wonderful sense of humor. She could not deny how much she really enjoyed spending time with him.

He caught her watching him and flashed that sexy grin, which caused a shudder to pass through her.

He watched as she struggled to finish her butternut-squash tortellini. "This is some of the best Italian food in California," he said as she put her cutlery down and pushed her half-finished plate aside.

It was, except Addison did not want to be stabbing pasta with a fork when her gaze could be held by his, and her mouth did not want to be eating when she could be speaking with him. The restaurant was suddenly too noisy, too busy, all distractions unwelcome.

"It is delicious," she agreed. "They just give you so much of it. I'm taking the rest of mine back to the hotel."

She shook her head when the waiter came over with a bottle of champagne, but he ignored her protest and poured two glasses.

"You ordered champagne?"

Kellen nodded. "We have something to celebrate."

"And what is that?"

"Friendship."

"You mean us?" she asked, surprised.

"Yes," Kellen responded. "I'd like for us to be friends, Addison. Don't worry. I'm clear on the boss thing."

"Okay, friend. So what else do you like besides football?"

"I love basketball, too," he said. "In fact, I love it more than football."

"Did you play?"

Kellen met her gaze. His eyes always did funny things to her stomach when they locked on hers.

He nodded and said, "I played both football and basketball all through high school and college."

"I played on the girls' basketball team in high school," Addison stated.

"I never figured you for a basketball player."

"Why? Is it because you think I'm way too girly?"

"Something like that," Kellen admitted with a chuckle. Addison knew that he was teasing her.

"I'm staying at the Alexander-DePaul Hotel. Where are you staying?" he asked after paying the bill.

"I'm staying there, too," she uttered. "I bet you're staying in one of those fabulous suites."

"I can have your room upgraded, if you'd like."

She shook her head. "My room is really nice. I'm fine."

Kellen checked his watch. "It's still early. Is there anything else you'd like to do?"

She shook her head. "I don't have anything in mind."

"We can maybe catch a movie somewhere?" The truth was that Kellen wasn't ready for the night to end. He was enjoying his time with Addison.

"Sounds good, but we have to go to the hotel first. I want to freshen up and change clothes."

She drove them to the hotel.

Kellen couldn't take his eyes off Addison.

"I can feel you staring at me."

"I was just admiring the view," he responded.

"You need to quit," Addison uttered with a short laugh.

"Okay," he said. "I'm going to behave."

"Yeah, right."

"Meet you at your room in about fifteen minutes," he said upon their arrival to the hotel.

Addison got off the elevator and headed to her room while Kellen went to his.

In his suite, he took a quick shower and changed into a fresh pair of jeans and a crisp linen shirt in a soft peach color. Kellen made a quick phone call to his dad.

Fifteen minutes passed.

Kellen waited another five before leaving his room and knocking on the door to Addison's hotel room.

She opened the door and exited with her purse. Addison

had changed into a pair of skinny jeans, a fuchsia-colored T-shirt and matching sandals.

They left the suite, walking down to the elevator.

The doors opened and they stepped inside.

"According to the desk clerk, the movie theater is not too far from here," Kellen stated.

"Do you want me to drive?" she asked. "We do have the rental car."

"You drove to the restaurant and back to the hotel," he said. "Let's just take a taxi."

"I'd rather take the car. I'm not crazy about taxicabs."

"Do you mind if I drive?"

"Not at all," Addison responded.

They made it to the movie theater in less than twenty minutes.

Kellen reached over and took her hand in his as they entered the theater. A warm feeling of well-being stole over her, and she found herself remembering the kindness and gentleness of Kellen's touch long after he released her hand.

"That was a great movie," Addison said when they returned to the hotel and relaxed in his suite.

When he didn't respond, she glanced over at him. "Kellen?"

"Huh?"

"What are you thinking about?"

His gaze landed on her face. "Do you really want to know?"

Addison thought she saw a whisper of something inviting in Kellen's eyes. It was a look that said he wouldn't mind a kiss, and she caught her breath as he half bent down toward her. For just a minute she felt like a young woman coming home from a date, her chest filled with the anticipation of a sweet first kiss with a promise of something more to come.

Addison quickly backed up.

She realized she wanted Kellen to kiss her, but she had to resist the temptation.

Addison wondered what his mouth would taste like, how his lips might play on her own. It would be the height of stupidity to allow a kiss to take place between them.

Yet she was powerless to resist.

His mouth covered hers hungrily.

A five-star kiss in a five-star hotel; his mouth soft and suggestive on her lips, his scent, the feel of his warm hands on her flushed cheeks. There was a moment where Kellen increased the pressure, where he shifted just a little and she felt as if they were both lost in the moment.

She returned his kiss with a hunger that belied her outward calm. Burying her face in his neck, Addison breathed a kiss there.

When the kiss ended, she resisted the urge to touch the place where his lips had been. Her heart was racing, and Addison could feel her blood rushing through her veins. She was falling for Kellen.

She looked into his eyes. She'd never been able to resist his eyes; she should have known better. But in the moment their eyes met, it was like she could hear him speaking, although his lips never moved.

Don't leave. Stay with me.

Silence fell, heavy with implications. Because neither of them was saying it had been a mistake. Or expressing regret. Or promising it would never happen again.

"Addison, I'm not a man to beat around the bush," Kellen blurted a moment later. "I'm very interested in you, and from that kiss, I believe that you feel the same way about me. I'd really like to see where this road takes us."

"A relationship can't happen between us," she interjected quickly. "Not as long as we're working together."

"Maybe you should fire me again."

Addison smiled. "Maybe I should."

"Why are you so against us being together?" he asked.

"I've never made it a habit to date someone I worked with," she responded. "If the relationship doesn't work out, then it carries over into the office. I don't want that."

"Like I told you before—I know how to separate my personal life from my business one."

"Kellen, we definitely have chemistry," she admitted. "But animal attraction burns itself out eventually."

"Is there anything I can do to change your mind?"

Addison reached over and took his hand in her own. "No, there isn't."

"I'm crazy about you."

She held her ground. "We can't do this."

He kissed her. "Are you sure?"

"I am," Addison stated. "Let's just keep it at friendship. Okay?"

Kellen snapped straight up and stepped back from her. "If that's what you want."

"Thank you," she whispered. "I think I'm going to call it a night."

"You're welcome to fly back with me," he told her. "We leave at six in the morning."

"I already have my ticket. I won't be in the office until noon tomorrow. I'll see you then."

Kellen walked her to the door.

"Good night, friend," she murmured.

Chapter 8

During the ride from the airport to the office, Kellen tried to erase the memory of their kiss. He had wanted to kiss her so badly, it had ached in his bones. Chest slowly squeezing the air from his lungs, he quickly reminded himself that he hadn't intentionally set out to have a casual fling with Addison, no matter how attractive she was.

More important, he wasn't trying to seduce her, either. Kellen had no desire to chase a woman who was throwing up caution signs all over the place. Addison was more of a road-totally-closed type of woman. But he wanted Addison, and the desire was so strong that it had him seriously considering making an exception.

Addison had promptly shut down the thought of a relationship, even though she enjoyed the kiss as much as he had. Kellen recalled in vivid detail how she moaned softly as his mouth slid from hers and dropped fleeting kisses on her cheeks, her eyes and the tip of her ear.

He knew exactly what was happening. He was falling in love with Addison.

Kellen had to find out if she felt the same way.

As soon as Addison arrived, he gave her enough time to get her day organized before going to see her.

She looked as if she had been waiting for him.

"I'm glad you're here," Addison began. "I enjoyed our time together yesterday in San Francisco, but I want to make sure that you understand I have no intentions of fast-tracking my career by sleeping with Malcolm Alexander's son."

"Glad to hear it," he responded.

"I like you, and I think…"

She barely got the words out of her mouth before his lips touched hers. Gently at first, his lips teased and tormented, until finally, Addison opened her mouth to encourage him to deepen the kiss.

And he did.

His arms tightened around her as the fire in his kiss stole her breath away. It had been so long, so achingly long since she'd felt wanted—it had been a long time since she'd wanted a man as much as she desired Kellen. He kissed her with a natural mastery that thrilled and surprised her.

He tenderly broke the kiss.

"Kellen…what are we doing?" Addison asked with a shake of her head.

"I wanted to be sure of your feelings for me," he murmured in response.

"We've been through this already, Kellen. We can't do this."

"Why not? Because of what other people may think?" he responded, looking confused. "It's clear that I want you, and you feel the same way."

"What it is—is inappropriate behavior," Addison uttered. "Kellen, listen to me. I can't get involved with you for several reasons, but the main reason is that I'm not willing to get involved with you. I'm sorry."

"I'll respect your wishes, Addison. I hope you won't hold it against me, but I just wanted to give it one more try. I really care about you."

"I care about you, as well...as a friend."

He gestured toward the door. "I have some work to do. I'd better get back to it."

Addison remembered all too well how good it felt to be held in Kellen's arms, the warmth and strength of his embrace comforting and yet enticing and exciting. The kisses they had shared had heated her body to the extent that she felt completely alive and whole, and all she'd been able to think about was the fire of his kiss, which warmed her from head to toe and left her wanting more of him.

He kept telling her that he had feelings for her. Addison wanted to believe him. The risk-taker in her continued to beg to be freed—she wanted to let go with Kellen and see where it led, but deep down she was afraid. She feared letting someone like him get close to her—someone who could distract her away from her goals.

She had done nothing but think of him lately, which is what Addison did not want to happen, but it was no use to pretend. She wanted him.

Falling in love with Kellen would be as easy as breathing, but Addison knew that certain heartbreak loomed ahead like a dark cloud. She could not afford to look in that direction. She had worked too hard to get to this place in her life. Her career meant everything to her, and Addison vowed nothing would keep her from her goal of upper-level management.

"I'm worried about Dreyden," Sage stated at the dinner table. She and her family had joined her parents and

Kellen for Sunday dinner. "I know that there's something wrong with him. He really doesn't look like himself at all."

Ryan agreed. "Honey, I'm sure if it were anything serious, Dreyden would've said something to you all."

Kellen wiped his mouth over the edge of his napkin. "Dreyden's lost a lot of weight, and it's not like he's losing it intentionally. Then his skin—it doesn't look right."

Barbara took a sip of iced tea before saying, "I must admit that I've been concerned about him, as well. I talked to him last night and he's promised to stop putting off seeing a doctor."

"He's been really stubborn about this," Sage stated. "I don't understand why."

"When I spoke with Dreyden earlier, he said he was calling the doctor after we hung up," Malcolm interjected. "I just hope that his doctor can see him soon."

Kellen checked his phone. "He just sent me a text. His appointment is on Friday morning. I think he sent it to you and Mom, too."

Barbara released a small sigh of relief. "This is good news."

"I just hope that it's nothing serious," Sage uttered.

"I don't think it is," Kellen responded. "Dreyden is the most health conscious of all of us."

Sage took a sip of her iced tea. "Except when it comes to seeing a doctor."

"He's hardly ever been sick." Kellen sliced off a piece of chicken and stuck it into his mouth.

"You both should have regular checkups," Barbara advised. "It's important to stay in tune with your body."

Kellen smiled but did not comment. He wasn't in the mood for a lecture on health and wellness.

"How are things going at the office?" Sage inquired as she reached for her water glass.

"Great," he responded. "Addison and I are getting along. Mostly, I'm enjoying the project I'm currently working on."

"That's good," Malcolm stated. "You've impressed everyone at the firm, from what I've been told."

Kellen was curious if Addison was the person his dad had spoken with, but decided not to ask.

Kellen began creating project stacks on his desk since he had been assigned to more projects. He had a routine of clearing his desk by Monday only to have stacks of projects by Friday. He always felt such a strong sense of satisfaction whenever he finished a task assignment. It was exhilarating.

His eyes traveled the length of his office. Ten rolls of onion-skin paper were stacked in one corner near a set of bookshelves. One side was filled with architectural reference books and manuals, while the other side held stacks of magazines he used for inspiration.

Whistling softly, Kellen picked up his master measure calculator. When it came to his projects, he never relied on his brain when adding up dimensions. One miscalculation could end up costing thousands of dollars.

He loved his job and had settled into his schedule comfortably.

"Here are the interior structures for the Arizona project," Kellen announced when he walked into Addison's office.

He sat quietly while she reviewed the rendering.

"Good work," Addison told him as she turned page after page. "Oh, what's this?"

He leaned forward. "That's just something I was working on. It wasn't supposed to be in there." Kellen had forgotten that he'd tossed all of his renderings into his portfolio last night before going to bed.

Addison eyed the drawing. "Kellen, this is great work," she said with a smile. "You know, I'm surprised you don't want to design buildings."

"I enjoy it, but I didn't want to just focus on the exterior. I also wanted to be able to design the interior, as well."

"You should show this to Jonathan. He's the lead architect on the Alexander-DePaul Hotels. I think he'd be interested in discussing it with you." She smiled again. "This is really nice."

Her words boosted his confidence. She believed in him.

Strangely, this mattered to Kellen. Addison was important to him, despite the fact that she wanted to remain friends. He cared for her more than he ever could have imagined possible.

Chapter 9

Kellen left work and drove straight to Dreyden's condo. The family had finally convinced or, according to Dreyden, *nagged* him to see his doctor. He was eager to find out how the appointment went.

"How did it go with the doctor?" he asked as soon as Dreyden opened the door.

"Hello to you, too."

"I'm sorry," Kellen responded. "I didn't mean to be rude. I just want to know what the doctor had to say."

"He gave me a physical and ordered some tests," Dreyden explained as they settled down in the living room. "He basically just asked about the nature of my symptoms and how long I've been experiencing them. He did feel some type of mass in my abdomen. That's why he ordered the lab work. I didn't get the impression that it was anything really serious. He did say that he might want me to see a specialist, depending on the results."

Kellen released a long sigh of relief. "I'm glad you

saw a doctor. I'm sure it's nothing serious, but we want to keep it that way."

Dreyden nodded in agreement. "I guess I should hear something back in a few days."

He studied his brother for a moment. "Let me know as soon as you hear."

"I will," Dreyden promised.

Kellen could not ignore the tiny wave of apprehension that washed over him. He wanted desperately to believe that there was nothing wrong with his brother. "Have you eaten?" he asked. "We can order something and have it delivered."

Dreyden waved his hand in dismissal. "Get something for you, but I'm not hungry."

"You have to eat something," Kellen stated. "You don't need to lose any more weight, bro. At this rate, you won't have a six-pack—it'll be more like a two-pack. Think about the effect that will have on your love life."

Dreyden chuckled. "I'm not looking for a wife, Kellen."

"Hey, you're next in line to get married. Mom already knows that it's the last thing on my mind. She hasn't given up on you, though."

"She did ask me if I was thinking about settling down."

Kellen burst into laughter. "See? I told you."

Dreyden tossed the remote to him. "Find something on television that's a lot more entertaining than you."

"Do any of you know why we've been called here?" Kellen asked a couple of days later. He met his parents outside of Dreyden's condo. "Did he get the results from his doctor?"

Malcolm shook his head. "He just called and requested our presence."

Sage and Ryan stepped off the elevator. They rushed over to join Kellen and their parents.

"What's going on?" she asked.

"We don't know," Kellen responded, ringing the doorbell. "It must be important, though."

His brother opened the door and stepped aside to let them enter.

"Dreyden…" Barbara began. "Honey, is everything okay?"

"I want to wait until everybody gets here."

Kellen tried to gauge his expression, but Dreyden had always been good about hiding his emotions.

They made small talk while they waited for the rest of the family members to arrive.

When everyone had arrived, Dreyden didn't keep them guessing. For a moment it seemed he was searching for the right words. Finally, he said, "I got the results back from my doctor."

Kellen met his gaze. "What did he have to say?"

"He found that my bile flow is blocked and that I have a mass in my abdomen. Dr. Winston referred me to an oncologist. I saw him this morning and he wants to have more tests done."

"Well, what kind of tests, son?" Malcolm asked.

"He wants to get more detailed images on the inside of my abdomen. They are doing a CT scan and an ultrasound. He even mentioned an MRI."

"That's a lot of tests," Sage commented, a worried expression on her face.

Are they saying you have cancer? Kellen wanted to know. His stomach was filled with apprehension. He wished they had been able to convince Dreyden to see a doctor sooner.

"Dr. Winston said that he wants me to have a biopsy."

Kellen's body went rigid. Before he could get the question out, his mother asked, "Does he think you have cancer?"

"The biopsy can confirm whether or not the mass is cancerous."

"Oh, Lord..." his mother murmured.

"Mom, it's going to be okay," Dreyden said. "This may turn into nothing."

"When is the biopsy scheduled?" Ari questioned.

"Friday morning."

Kellen shook his head. "You can't have cancer." He refused to believe that something like this could happen to his brother. He was in great shape despite the past few weeks.

"This is my wish," Dreyden stated. "I'm hoping that they won't find anything, but if they do—I hope that it's in the very early stages."

"I hope so, too," he responded. Kellen thought about the months of nagging Dreyden just to see the doctor. He hoped his brother was going to be fine. No one in his family had ever been directly affected by cancer, so this was new to them.

Malcolm got up and placed a hand on Dreyden's shoulder. "We will get through this, no matter what."

They all agreed.

Kellen tried not to show it, but he was afraid for his brother.

"Kellen, what's wrong?" Addison inquired as soon as he walked through the glass double doors early the next morning. "You look terrible." He was usually in a good mood whenever he arrived, but today was different.

"Right now, I'd have to say that's a whole lot better than I feel," he responded without emotion. "I had a bad night."

She stood in his path. "Do you want to talk about it?

We can go into my office." Addison was concerned as she'd never seen him like this.

He shook his head. "Thanks, but I'll be okay. I just need to get to work."

"I have a better idea. Why don't you take the day off?" Addison suggested. "Go home and try to get some rest."

"No, I would rather stay here," Kellen responded. "I really need to stay busy."

She surveyed his face. "Are you sure?"

"Yeah," he answered.

Kellen turned away from Addison and headed toward his office.

Inside, he dropped his backpack on his desk and opened it, removing the laptop.

He walked around the desk and sat down, facing the monitor.

Addison watched him for a moment from the hallway before navigating back to her office. He was always in a cheerful mood, but now he looked so sad, and it really bothered her seeing him this way.

Kellen stayed in his office most of the day.

She checked on him around lunchtime. "Are you hungry?"

"Not really," he responded.

"You have to eat sometime," Addison reminded him. "Why don't I order something from the deli on the next block and have it delivered?"

"Sure, that's fine. Thanks, Addison."

"No problem."

She left his office a few minutes later.

Addison returned after his lunch had been delivered. "Here's your food. I want you to eat it."

"I never realized just how bossy you really are," Kellen murmured.

She smiled. "Only when I need to be."

"Kellen, I don't know what's happened, but I can see that it's really bothering you."

"This is something I've never had to encounter, Addison. For the first time in a very long time—I'm scared."

She couldn't imagine what could possibly scare a man like Kellen, but whatever it was—it had to be something really bad.

Addison placed a gentle hand on his shoulder. "I'm here if you need me, Kellen."

He covered her hand with his own. "Thank you."

The bond she shared with him had deepened because Addison could feel his pain.

"Dreyden had a biopsy this morning," Kellen announced two days later. "He hasn't been feeling well for the past few months. He went to the doctor and they ran a bunch of tests, but we don't know anything for sure until the results of the biopsy come through." He shook his head sadly. "Addison, I haven't said this to my family, but I have a really bad feeling about this."

"I'm so sorry," she murmured. She resisted the urge to wrap her arms around him and offer comfort. "Your brother is a really nice man. Kellen, it could turn out to be nothing at all."

"I hope that you're right."

"I can see that you're really worried about him."

Kellen nodded. "Dreyden's always been healthy. He was hardly sick when we were growing up, so this is something I'm not used to. Addison, he's lost so much weight."

"Why don't you go to him? Go be with your brother."

He gave her a tight smile. "Thank you, Addison. I'm taking my laptop with me. I'll work from his place."

"I hope everything works out for the best for Dreyden."

"Thanks for your understanding," Kellen told her. "Nothing is more important to me than my family."

"I understand completely," Addison murmured. "I'll keep your brother in my prayers."

"I'm sure he will appreciate it as much as I do." He packed up his laptop. "I'll give you a call later."

She smiled and nodded.

Kellen practically ran to his car. He wanted to be there for Dreyden. Checking his watch, he knew that his parents had driven him home where he could recuperate in bed for the rest of the day.

"What are you doing here?" Dreyden asked drowsily when Kellen strode into his bedroom. "You're supposed to be working."

"I came to see how you were doing," Kellen responded. "Not that I was worried or anything."

Dreyden gave a tiny smile. "That's because there's nothing to worry about, little brother."

"Knock knock…"

Kellen glanced over his shoulder to see Sage standing in the doorway. He smiled as she joined them inside. "Hey, sis."

She hugged Dreyden and then Kellen. "I thought you were going into work today."

"I did, but I couldn't focus," he confessed. "I wanted to be here."

"Same here," Sage contributed. She looked at Dreyden and said, "All I could think about was you."

"What's up with you two? Why are y'all hovering over me like this? It's not that serious."

Before either of them could respond, their parents walked into the room, followed by Ari.

"Is *anybody* working today? I don't want you all sitting around my house like this," Dreyden stated. "I said that I'd call y'all if I got any news."

"Stop your fussing and get some rest," Sage ordered.

They sat in the living room while he slept.

Kellen sat with his hands curled into fists. All this waiting…he hated it.

"I can't take much more of this," Sage said in a low voice. "I need to know what we're up against."

"What Dreyden is up against," Ari corrected.

"Whatever he's going through will affect this family as a whole," Kellen interjected. "If he does have cancer, our family will never be the same."

"We are not going to fall apart, Kellen. This family is stronger together."

"Dreyden was always the strong one," he responded in a low voice.

Chapter 10

A couple of days later, Dreyden, Kellen and their parents sat in a waiting room.

"I'm ready to get this over with," Dreyden uttered. "They wouldn't tell me anything over the phone."

Barbara reached over and gave his hand a gentle squeeze.

The nurse opened a door and called out, "Dreyden Alexander."

"I want my family with me," he told her.

She smiled and stepped aside to let them enter.

"What we found is neuroendocrine cell tumors," Dr. Walton explained after they were seated in his office. "This is the cause of your abdominal pain and weight loss. After looking at your test results, I'm surprised that you haven't had any attacks of acute pancreatitis in the past."

Kellen glanced over at his brother. Dreyden never complained of pain, but then it was not his nature.

"Can you please tell us what is wrong with our son?" Barbara asked. "Are the tumors cancerous?"

"Yes," Dr. Walton responded.

"He has pancreatic cancer." Barbara glanced up at her husband. "Malcolm…" Her words died as she leaned against him for support.

"P-pancreatic cancer," Kellen repeated, complete disbelief on his face. "Are you sure about this, Doctor? How could this happen?"

"Pancreatic cancer develops when a cell in the pancreas acquires damage to its DNA that causes it to behave and multiply abnormally," Dr. Walton explained. "A single cancer cell grows and divides rapidly, becoming a tumor that does not respect normal boundaries in the body. Eventually, cells from the tumor travel elsewhere in the body through the blood or lymphatic system. When enough mutations accumulate, a cell becomes malignant and a tumor begins to grow."

"My brother has cancer," Sage murmured. "That's what you're telling us?"

Kellen embraced her. "He's going to be fine. Dreyden, we're going to fight this together."

Dreyden eyed his doctor. "What is the extent of my cancer?"

"We really won't know exactly how far the cancer has spread until surgery," Dr. Walton confirmed.

"Okay, so when are you going to do the surgery?"

"I'd like to schedule it for Monday morning."

"I don't have anything on my schedule," Dreyden said with a tiny smile.

It isn't right.

After the surgery, Dr. Walton found that the cancer had spread to other organs.

Kellen and his family had all gone in believing that

any cancerous tumors would be removed and this nightmare would end.

This was not the case, however. His heart dropped as he listened to the oncologist explaining that the tumors could not be safely removed because other organs were affected. Dr. Walton was able to remove the obstruction found, but announced that there was nothing else he could do.

Stage IV cancer.

It just didn't feel real. There was no way Dreyden had stage IV pancreatic cancer. He was full of life. His brother had everything to live for.

Dreyden was taking it all in stride.

Kellen supposed it could be the medication he was on, but then again, he always presented a calm front. He was relieved when Dreyden agreed to start chemotherapy.

He felt like smashing his fist into a wall. Kellen was that angry and he wanted to hit something. Anything.

Ari walked over and stood beside him. "Believe me, I know how you feel."

He turned to face his oldest brother. "Were you this angry when April got sick?"

"Yes," he responded. "Perhaps even angrier."

Kellen shook his head sadly. "I feel like this is some cruel joke." He dropped his arm to his side and looked at Ari. "I feel helpless. That's my brother lying in that bed and I can't do anything to help him."

"I know," Ari replied. "He's my brother, too."

Kellen raised his eyes upward. *God, were you listening to me? I need Dreyden to get well. We can't lose him.*

He felt his father's hand on his arm. Their gazes met.

Shaking his head sadly, Kellen released a long sigh. Shifting against the wall, his movements were now stiff as he braced himself for battle. Only this was a fight he might not win.

* * *

"Is there something going on between you and Kellen?" Tia asked as Addison put away her cell phone in her beach tote. They were spending the afternoon at Venice Beach.

She turned to face her friend. "Why would you ask me something like that?"

"I've noticed that you just seem to have a special way of lighting up whenever you mention his name."

"He is a really nice guy, Tia," she said. "But I'm his boss, and don't forget that I'm five years older than he is."

"I don't think any of that matters to anyone but you, Addison. This may be the man for you."

"I doubt it."

"I think you two would make a cute couple."

Her arms folded across her chest, Addison inquired, "Why are you suddenly advocating for this man? You don't know anything about him outside of what you've read in some magazine or newspaper."

"I've seen the way you two look at each other." Tia smiled at her friend. "C'mon, Addison. Can you look me in the face and tell me that you have no feelings for Kellen Alexander?"

Addison took a sip of her tea. "Okay, so I'm very attracted to him, but as I told you before—I'm not going to act on it."

"Office romances happen. The only thing I would say is that you have to be able to separate your business relationship from a personal one."

She laughed. "It's not going to happen, Tia."

"Two years from now, I don't want to hear all of your regrets."

"Okay, we can change the subject."

Addison sat her tote down on the beach towel and then

stared at the ocean. She craved the feel of the ocean air on her skin. She quickly put her hair up in a ponytail. "I'm going for a swim. Are you joining me?"

Fifteen minutes before her alarm clock was set to go off, Addison lay in the dark, her thoughts of her mother and how much she missed her. She wished more than anything that she could hear her mother's laughter once more, see her beloved face wreathed with a smile just one last time. Addison wished she could tell her mother about her new promotion and that she was doing well and was happy. That had been her mother's only concern during her illness—she worried about Addison, but there was no need.

She was strong. She had survived her mother's death, after all.

Her thoughts drifted to Kellen. She could tell that he was extremely worried about his brother. Addison hoped all was well with Dreyden.

She turned off the blaring alarm and climbed out of bed. It was time to start off the day with a thirty-minute workout.

Afterward, Addison showered and dressed.

"Hey, how's Dreyden doing?" Addison asked as she entered Kellen's office an hour later.

She paused in her steps when he did not respond to her question.

"Did you hear me?" she prompted.

Kellen nodded, and then turned around in his chair to meet her steady gaze. "I'm afraid it's not good news, Addison. We found out that Dreyden has pancreatic cancer."

"Nooo," she uttered. "Kellen...I'm so sorry."

"I keep telling myself that this is not happening. My

brother can't have cancer," he muttered. "Dreyden's the most health-conscious of all of my siblings. I just don't see how this can happen to him."

Addison shook her head sadly. "I don't know. I just hate to see you going through this—you or your family." She sat down beside him. "The thing is…Kellen, you cannot lose faith. I'm not going to get superspiritual on you, but God has the final say."

"I know that, and I don't believe that my brother's going to die or anything," Kellen stated. "I'm just finding it hard to believe that we are even dealing with this."

"How are you holding up?"

Kellen looked up from his work. "I'm good, thanks, which is mostly because of you. Addison, I wanted to thank you again for talking me down this morning. You said all the right things and I really appreciate it."

"I meant what I said. I will be here for you. Oh, I have something for you." She pulled a photograph out of her purse. "I found this when I was going through some boxes containing old records that were in storage."

"It's a picture of my grandfather," Kellen stated. "From what I hear, my father shares many of Robert's qualities. I suppose working in the hotel industry is in their blood. You know Robert had been in the hotel business since he was old enough to carry luggage. My dad has pretty much the same background. His family has managed a couple of hotels in Georgia for several generations."

"I heard that Robert met Malcolm's mother when he opened the hotel in Wilmington, North Carolina. She worked there as a housekeeper."

Kellen nodded. "It's true. Obviously, they could not control their feelings for one another. You can't help who you fall in love with."

"I'm not sure I agree with that statement," Addison

stated. "I think it's natural to develop feelings for someone you work with closely, but that you have to learn to control those feelings. Besides, most of the work romances that I know about have turned out badly."

"Ari and Natalia met on the job and fell in love," Kellen stated. "So did Sage and Ryan."

"I thought he was a journalist."

"He is, but he worked undercover for us—that's how they met. Blaze and Livi didn't meet on the job, but they reconnected at work."

"What about your other sister?" Addison inquired. "Zaire."

"She met her husband on the job, as well—they are business partners."

"Apparently, this is some kind of trend in your family," she said with a smile. "It started with Robert De-Paul, apparently."

"I suppose we are going to break tradition."

"Why don't we get out of here and grab some lunch?" Addison suggested, changing the subject.

"I'm not hungry."

"We've been through this already. I'll say it again. You have to eat something," she insisted.

Kellen shook his head. "Can I have a rain check?"

"I can bring something back for you if you don't feel like going out."

He smiled at her. "Thanks, but I'll be okay."

"I wish there was something more I could do for you," Addison said in earnest. She knew exactly what he was going through. She had experienced those same emotions when her mother was first diagnosed with breast cancer. She didn't want to believe it, either.

"They've made great strides in cancer research," Kellen was saying, trying to see his brother's condition in a positive light. "Dreyden's strong. He can beat this. My nephew is in remission from leukemia. If we all stick together we can beat this dreadful disease."

Addison listened because that's what Kellen needed at the moment. He just needed someone to listen.

Chapter 11

Kellen stayed with Dreyden at the condo after his first round of chemotherapy. He brought his laptop with him and worked while his brother slept.

Ari was looking into clinical trials while his parents wanted the best oncologist in the world treating Dreyden.

"You should eat," Kellen said. He recalled Addison telling him the same thing just the day before.

He nodded but didn't move toward the bowl on the table next to him.

His thick lashes fluttered up, his gaze blurry. "Sorry, I'm so incredibly exhausted."

"It's all right. I'll feed you. Here." He lifted the bowl of soup, steam rising into the air and bringing with it the comforting scent of chicken and noodles. He pressed the spoon to Dreyden's lips.

His brother rested his pale hand on his stomach, drawing attention to the dips of muscle.

When he finished feeding Dreyden, Kellen cleaned up the kitchen.

He found his brother sleeping so he settled down in the living room to watch some television. He stayed there until he heard Dreyden calling out to him. His voice was weak but audible.

"I'm… I don't feel w-well…"

Kellen helped him to the bathroom.

Dreyden fell to his knees with his head over the toilet.

"It's going to be all right," he whispered as he placed a cold washcloth to his brother's forehead. "You're going to be fine."

He helped Dreyden back to bed, but only after his brother insisted on brushing his teeth.

"Take a few sips of water," Kellen advised. "If you prefer, I can get you some ice chips."

Dreyden shook his head. "Water's fine."

He sat in the chair near the bed. "Do you want to watch some television? I think there's a game on."

"You go ahead."

Kellen's eyes teared up as he surveyed his brother in this weakened state. He blinked rapidly. He didn't want to let Dreyden see him cry. He had to be strong.

His brother needed him and Kellen was not going to let him down.

"You seem kind of down," Tia observed aloud as they left the movie theater. "Is something bothering you?"

"One of my employees received some bad news. They have a really sick family member."

"I hope things get better," Tia said. "Did you know him or her?"

"I met him," she responded. "And I'm praying things work out for the best."

"I think it's really nice the way that you care about

your employees. My manager is just the opposite." Tia made a face. "I don't think I told you, but I've decided to look for another job. I've already sent my résumé and portfolio to several companies."

Addison broke into a grin. "Good for you, Tia. It's about time. You're a great interior decorator. I'm sure you'll find something quick."

"I know that you've been telling me for years to do this, but I stayed because I wanted to build up my experience."

She nodded in understanding.

Addison picked up the phone with the intent to call Kellen later that evening. She changed her mind and went back to the work she'd brought home with her.

However, she couldn't stop thinking about Kellen. Addison changed her mind once more and grabbed her cell phone.

"I just wanted to call and check on you," Addison said when Kellen answered.

"I'll be okay," he told her. "It's just been a lot to take in."

She noted that he did not sound like himself at all. Addison's heart fell as she heard the despair in his voice. "It doesn't sound like you feel like talking so I won't keep you. I just wanted to check to see how you are doing."

"Thank you."

"If you ever want to talk, please call me." Addison wanted to say more but couldn't. She had set the terms of their relationship. She could not change things now.

"Hey, big brother…" Kellen called out as he entered Dreyden's condo, using the extra key. "Where are you?"

"I'm in here."

He followed his brother's voice to the master bedroom. "I hope I didn't wake you," Kellen stated when he walked inside.

Dreyden was sitting up in bed with his back propped against a stack of pillows. "I've been up for a while."

"I overheard Dad telling Ari that your partners are buying you out."

Dreyden nodded as he plumped the pillows on his bed. "Yeah, they are. I think it's the best thing to do, considering my circumstances."

Kellen met his brother's gaze. "So you're retiring? When did you decide this?"

"I guess you can call it retirement," his brother answered.

"What do you call it?" Kellen asked.

"I consider it putting all of my affairs in order."

"I don't want to hear you talking like that, Dreyden," he responded quickly. *"You are not going to die."*

Dreyden released a soft sigh. "As scary as it sounds, we have to be realistic, Kellen."

He shook his head. "No, I don't. I'm not listening to this."

Kellen strode quickly to the floor-to-ceiling window and stared out. "I'm sorry, but death is not an option."

"Hey, I'm not afraid to die," Dreyden stated. "I've made my peace with the Lord. I just know that I'm going to miss you and the rest of the family."

Kellen walked over to the bed and sat down on the left side near the footboard. "Why are you just giving up?"

"I'm not giving up."

"If you think you're going to die," Kellen uttered, "then you're giving up."

"I intend to live as long as I have breath in my body," Dreyden stated. "Trust me when I tell you that I'm fighting to live, little brother, but I have to be prepared either way."

"Just so you know, death is not an option," Kellen repeated. "You are going to be rid of this cancer, so that you can find that perfect woman and get married. I'm going to dance at your wedding."

Dreyden laughed, but it was weak at best.

"How are things going with Addison?" Dreyden asked, deliberately changing the subject.

Kellen nodded. "I have to admit that she's a spitfire when she wants to be. However, I was able to convince her to give me another chance."

"You really like her," Dreyden said.

Kellen smiled. "She's all right."

"Who are you trying to kid?"

"Okay, I like her. She's beautiful. Who wouldn't like a woman like that?"

Dreyden nodded in agreement. "Have you asked her out?"

"Once," Kellen responded. "She turned me down flat. Addison doesn't believe in dating her employees."

"It can be a sticky situation."

"I guess," Kellen muttered.

"Does it still bother you that she's your boss?" Dreyden wanted to know.

He shook his head.

His brother clearly didn't believe him. "Liar."

"It bothers me because I have strong feelings for Addison. I don't even know how or when it happened."

"I wish I could say that I'm surprised by this, but I'm not," Dreyden responded.

He sounded so exhausted.

"I'm going in the living room so that you can get some rest," Kellen announced. "Call me if you need anything."

Dreyden was already half asleep.

Although Dreyden hadn't told them how much time the doctor gave him, Kellen suspected that it wasn't long.

He noticed that his brother had progressive weakness and exhaustion. Dreyden was continuing to lose weight and had little or no appetite. All of the material he'd read suggested that his brother was entering the final weeks of his life.

Kellen understood that every person was different, which is why he continued to hold on to hope and pray fervently for the Lord to heal Dreyden. He refused to give up on a miracle—they happened every day.

"Please don't take my brother," he whispered. "He loves You and is a good man. He deserves to live and grow old. He deserves to find love and get married—raise a family. Lord, my brother deserves all of these things. Please save him."

Chapter 12

The stark light of morning sunshine streaming through the nearby window pulled Kellen from a fitful night of sleep and into the glare of his harsh reality.

Dreyden was gone.

He had peacefully stepped out of time, passing into eternity shortly after 8:00 p.m. last evening.

Kellen sat up in bed, thinking back over the past four months.

He had witnessed Dreyden's rapid decline as death drew closer. Fatigue had taken over. His brother once told him, "I feel like an engine running out of steam. There are days that I have just enough energy to do one or two small things, and then it's gone. It's like I've used up my supply for that day. I'm getting tired of being tired."

The doctor had explained to the family that this was normal and a symptom with advanced cancer. He also told him that needing more sleep was also normal in the last few weeks of life.

Tears welled up in Kellen's eyes.

My brother is dead.

I'll never hear his voice again.

I can never come to him for advice or just to hang out.

Dreyden's last week or so had been filled with persistent pain. He had confided in Kellen, saying, "I need the morphine to do the things I want to do. I just hate spending my days flat on my back in bed."

A soft knock on the door cut into his thoughts.

"Come in."

Ari entered his bedroom. "I came to check on you."

Kellen gave a slight nod. "How are you holding up?"

She sat down on the edge of the king-size bed. "I keep thinking about Dreyden and wondering if we did everything we could to try and save him."

"We talked to the top oncologists in the world," Kellen stated. "We did everything."

They were joined a few minutes later by Sage and Zaire.

Zaire made herself comfortable beside him in bed, while Sage sat down on the nearby sofa.

"Has anyone seen Mom or Dad?" Sage inquired. "I didn't hear anything when I walked by their room."

"I hope that they're sleeping," Zaire responded. "They need to rest."

"Are we having a sibling meeting?" Blaze asked from the doorway.

"Come join us," Kellen said. "We're just in here talking."

Blaze sat down beside Sage.

They all sat in silence, each in their own thoughts.

"I knew Dreyden was leaving us when he couldn't eat much," Zaire blurted. "I read that when a person dies, their body goes through a series of changes that have an effect on their appetite. It's because of the drug side-effects and bodily function issues that make it hard for them to eat."

"I thought he was giving up," Kellen said. "I didn't know."

"Neither did I," Blaze responded. "I kept trying to force food down his throat."

"Dreyden didn't want pity," Sage stated. "He kept a lot of what he was dealing with to himself. That's just the way he was."

They all agreed.

"What do we do now?" Zaire asked. "I feel as if a part of me is missing."

Blaze nodded in agreement. "I was telling Livi that same thing this morning. As much as I love my family, my heart is broken at the thought of never seeing Dreyden again."

"He's our brother," Ari said. "It's normal to feel this type of heartache over a loss. Unfortunately, death is a part of life."

"I never want to go through anything like this again," Blaze uttered. "Watching my brother die... I can't put into words what I'm feeling."

"It was distressing for me in the last week because Dreyden's breathing changed," Zaire stated.

"Like Zaire, I knew what was coming because it sounded like he was drowning when he was breathing," Sage interjected. "It was so labored. It scared me."

Zaire agreed. "I think at times, it scared him, too." A lone tear rolled down her cheek. "I would take his hand and just rub it so that he knew he wasn't alone."

Kellen felt his own eyes grow wet. He and his siblings had all taken turns staying with Dreyden, so that he was never alone. His parents had had him transported via ambulance to the house in Pacific Palisades and hired a couple of private nurses to care for him around the clock. They were all present at the moment he took his very last breath.

Sage wiped away her tears. "This isn't fair."

"Life never is," Ari muttered.

Kellen knew that he was thinking about April, his first wife. She died shortly after their marriage and it had taken him some time to get over her death.

"We thought we'd find you in here," Malcolm said from the doorway. Barbara was with him. "Livi and Natalia are downstairs making breakfast for us. Why don't we all go down and try to eat something?"

"I need to wash up first," Kellen said. "I'll be down in a bit."

After everyone left his room, he decided it was time to give Addison the news. "Good morning. I just wanted to let you know that Dreyden passed away last night."

"Kellen, I'm so sorry…" Her voice broke. "How are you doing?"

"Right now…things are… I have to go, but I wanted to tell you before you heard it from someone else."

"Okay."

"I'll keep you posted on everything." He ended the call.

It was eight-forty when Kellen finally left the bathroom, freshly showered and dressed in a pair of fleece navy blue pants and a white-and-navy T-shirt.

Franklin was in the foyer when he reached the bottom floor. He had been in New York visiting his daughter when he heard about Dreyden. He was considered a member of the family, although he worked as the head of security for the Alexanders.

The two men embraced.

"I'm so sorry for your loss, Kellen. I knew how close you and Dreyden were."

"I know how much you loved him, too."

Franklin nodded. "I sure don't understand this at all."

"I don't think I ever will," Kellen muttered. "I feel like God turned His ear from me when I was praying for Him to heal my brother. He turned His back on Drey. What have I done that God doesn't listen to my p___ anymore?"

"He hears the prayers of His people," Frankli___ ___ him. "But for reasons we may never understa___ ___ times He says no."

It rained that Friday, the day of Dreyden'___ ___. The day was dull and dreary, matching Keller ___ d as he dressed in a black suit. He stared at his r___ ___ n in the mirror, blinking back tears.

A knock on his bedroom door dre___ ___m out of his reverie.

"Come in."

Ari opened the door and entered ___ came up to check on you."

"I'm okay," Kellen responded ___ ___ly.

"I know that you're not okay,"___ ___s brother responded. "None of us are doing well wit___ ___is."

"I dread walking into that c___ ___h and seeing Dreyden lying in that coffin."

"It's not easy, but this is t___ ___ly chance we have left to say goodbye to our broth___

"That's just it, Ari. I'm ___ ___ ready to say goodbye."

"Neither am I."

"Our family is never ___ ___ing to be the same," he said. "I'm not sure we can re___ over from this."

"I felt the same way ___ ___en I lost April," Ari responded. "It took a long time, ___ ___ now it doesn't hurt as much. I hated seeing Dreyde___ ___ pain—this is the only thing that gives me a measure ___ comfort about his death. He's no longer in pain. He's free."

"I know that you're right, but it doesn't make me feel any better."

Their father stuck his head inside. "The limos are here. We're leaving in five minutes."

"We're ready," Ari said, speaking for the two of them.

Kellen buttoned up his suit jacket and followed Ari out of the room. They joined the rest of the family downstairs in the living room.

His mother looked beautiful in a chic black dress with matching coat and a wide-brim black-and-white hat. Her purse and shoes were both black with white trim. She tried to give him a brave smile but failed.

Her sisters were seated side by side on the sofa. Zaire rubbed her swollen belly as her husband, Tyrese, rubbed her shoulders.

Livi walked up to him. "Let me redo your tie."

"It wasn't acting right today," he mumbled, glad for the help.

All of the children, except Joshua, were staying at the house with a babysitter. Joshua insisted on attending the home-going services. He adored Dreyden.

The funeral director escorted his parents out first, holding a large black umbrella over their heads.

They were soon in the cars and on their way to the church.

Kellen stared out the window, although nothing captured his interest. Images of him and his siblings when they were kids formed in his mind. Playing together, laughing one moment and then arguing the next. Dreyden was always the peacemaker. An unconscious smile formed on his lips.

At the front of the church, surrounded by floral arrangements sent from all over the country, was Dreyden's coffin, which was made of solid, natural-brush stainless steel. Column corners and swing-bar handles complemented the design. Full white-velvet interior surrounded his brother as he lay on the inner bed. His parents had spared no expense for their beloved son, but it was tasteful and elegant.

Kellen had no idea that Addison was in the congregation until he walked up to the podium to speak. He met her gaze briefly before turning his attention to the coffin below.

His voice threatened to break. Kellen cleared his throat. "My brother...Dreyden... There's so much that was special about him." He fought back tears. "He was a lot like our father: intelligent, supportive and he had a great sense of humor. Whenever I needed a reality check, he was the one to do it. He kept me on the straight and narrow."

A lone tear flowed down his cheek. "I don't think I'll ever understand why he had to leave us."

Kellen was joined by Ari and Blaze at the podium. It took him a moment to realize that he had stopped talking and was sobbing.

Ari embraced him.

"We will all miss Dreyden," Blaze said. "He left this earth much too soon, but his legacy will live on forever. My brother was generous to a fault and spent most of his free time finding ways to help others."

Kellen allowed his tears to run free as he made his way back to his seat. The thought of never hearing his brother's voice or seeing him again ripped through his heart.

"Addison, thank you for coming," Kellen said after the burial in the cemetery. The repast was held at his parents' house.

He glanced away to keep her from seeing his tears.

"I liked your brother," Addison responded softly as

she handed him a tissue. "He was a really nice guy and he'll be greatly missed."

He nodded in agreement.

"You don't have to hide your tears, Kellen. You just lost your brother."

He wiped at his eyes. "Are you coming to the house?"

Addison shook her head. "I would love to, but I need to head back to the office for a meeting. I'll give you a call later to check up on you."

"I'll walk you to your car," he murmured. "I need to get out of here for a few minutes."

Kellen reached over, taking her hand in his own. He needed her strength because his own was waning. "I want you to know that I really appreciate you being here, Addison."

"I wouldn't be anywhere else," she responded. "Kellen, I'm sure you're tired of hearing this, but I'm so deeply sorry for your loss."

"I never thought we'd end up in this place. I really didn't think he would...he wouldn't be here."

She embraced him.

"This just doesn't feel like my life."

"The grieving process is going to take some time," Addison whispered. "I'll call you later. If you don't feel like talking, I'll understand."

Kellen gave a slight nod.

"It was nice of Addison to come to the service," Zaire said after he walked back into the house. "She seems to care a great deal about you."

Kellen shrugged in nonchalance. "She's just being kind."

She looped her arm through his. "What are we going to do without Dreyden? My daughter will not ever get to meet him."

"We're going to tell her all about her uncle," he responded, his voice breaking. "She'll know how much he loved her and how much he wanted to be here when she was born."

Chapter 13

Addison looked out the window at the rain running down the pane. For a moment she paused, watching as lightning forked across the sky. It was a lackluster day at best and it matched her mood.

She could not forget the image of Kellen standing before his brother's coffin, his eyes filled with tears. Her own eyes watered at the memory. Losing a family member was never easy, but the pain she saw in the faces of the Alexanders nearly broke her heart.

With a sigh, Addison left the window in her bedroom to change into a pair of jeans and a snug, white T-shirt with a red heart on the front. She gathered her hair into a careless ponytail, the black ends touching the top of her spine.

The day crawled by. Addison was up to her ears in paperwork. She had gone over everything, crossing t's and dotting i's, making sure that not a single detail fell through the cracks.

Kellen stayed at the forefront of her mind. She wanted to check on him but didn't want to be a pest or give him the wrong idea.

Her heart refused to cooperate.

Addison picked up the phone and punched in Kellen's number.

"I'm just calling to check on you," she told him when he answered his phone.

"I'm still numb."

"You will probably feel this way for a while," she stated. "When I first realized my mother was terminally ill and her death was imminent, I didn't want to believe it. Soon after, I just didn't feel anything anymore. When she died, I was numb for a few months. After that there were days when I wasn't sure that I would make it through to the next one."

"How did you get through it?"

"My father and my brother were very supportive. My best friend, Tia, was great. After my mother died, I didn't even want to get out of bed, but she would come over, throw open the blinds to let sunlight inside… I would get so angry with her, but she refused to let me just check out on life. I still miss her like crazy, but Kellen, I can tell you that what you're feeling is normal. It will take time, but the pain you're feeling right now will lessen eventually."

"I don't know about that," he responded. "I don't think I'll ever feel normal again."

"You will," Addison assured him. "In time."

"I picked up the phone a few minutes ago to call Dreyden. Then I remembered that he's gone and won't be coming back."

A shrill scream pulled Kellen from his bed the next morning. He banged on the alarm clock, trying to shut it off.

He made his way downstairs and out to the patio. It seemed he was the only one awake at the moment. He sat listening to the ocean, while trying to drown out the silence.

Barbara joined him a few minutes later.

"I miss Dreyden," Kellen uttered, breaking the silence. "I can't bear the idea of him lying in that cold grave. He should be alive and well."

His mother reached over and gave his hand a gentle squeeze. "I know, baby. This is one of the worst things I've ever had to face…losing a child. It's hard, but we will get through this."

"It's just not fair," he argued. "Dreyden had so much to live for—he deserved to live, get married and have a family. He deserved to grow old."

"God obviously had another plan for him," Malcolm interjected. "Although I don't understand why He allowed death to take my son, I am grateful that Dreyden did not suffer too long."

"I'm angry."

"Honey, your brother is in a better place."

"That's what people say to try and make you feel better. But it's not working for me."

"How was the funeral?" Tia asked. "It looked like there were hundreds of people in attendance."

"There were," Addison confirmed as she picked up her menu. "It was a beautiful service. I just felt so bad for Malcolm Alexander and his family. Kellen was heartbroken. He could hardly talk without crying."

"The family seems really close."

"They are very close and this has been hard on all of them." Addison took a sip of her iced tea. "It brought back a lot of the emotions I felt when my mom died."

"I figured it might."

"I miss her so much but the pain has lessened over the years. This is still so new for Kellen and his family. It's so hard on them. I wish there was something I could do."

"Have you talked to Kellen since the funeral?"

"I check on him every day. He's grieving and he's angry."

"Just continue to be there for him."

"He told me that he's going to pack up Dreyden's condo this weekend. His brothers wanted to help, but he refused them—he wants to do it himself. Ari and Blaze are going to have it cleaned and painted so they can sell it."

"Maybe you should go over there and help him," Tia suggested.

"I was actually thinking about that," Addison confessed. "I feel like it's a bad idea for him to try and do this alone."

"I agree."

She nodded. "I've decided. I'm not going to let Kellen deal with this alone."

Chapter 14

Kellen spent the morning clearing out Dreyden's bedroom. He missed the sound of his brother's voice, and his strength. Oh, what he wouldn't give for that wisdom now, to sit here in this condo talking and working through it.

A knock on the door cut into his thoughts.

He walked in quick strides to answer it.

"Hey, what are you doing here?" Kellen asked in surprise. The last person he expected to see standing there was Addison.

"I knew that you were planning to be here today, so I thought I'd come help you." She broke into a smile. "That's what friends do."

"Come on in."

She followed him to the bedroom. "I started in here. Dreyden wanted us to take all of his clothes to the center. I just finished packing up his shoes."

"I'll start with his clothes," Addison said as she grabbed an empty box.

He watched her for a moment before returning to the task at hand.

After packing away all of the clothes, Addison made her way to the linen closet.

She packed the linens and towels while Kellen concentrated on the items in the dresser.

They took a break shortly after 2:00 p.m.

Kellen ordered a pizza.

They sat down to eat after it arrived.

"I'm close to all of my siblings, but Dreyden and I… we were friends."

Addison took a sip of her soda. "My family and I have never been that close, but I know how you feel. I would be devastated if I lost any of them."

"I'm so angry," Kellen confessed.

"Anger is a natural part of the grieving process. It's okay," she assured him.

"When does the acceptance part come?" he asked.

"It varies person to person."

When they finished eating, Kellen assessed and photographed each piece of furniture in the house for potential listing on eBay or valuation by a dealer, while Addison was assigned the task of cataloging the items.

"You didn't want to keep anything for yourself?" she asked.

He shook his head. "I have his watch collection. We all decided that it was best to sell the condo and furnishings. The proceeds are going to Dreyden's favorite charity."

"That's very sweet," she murmured.

"It's what he would've wanted. He left this place to me, but I could never live here," Kellen stated. "Just too many memories."

Addison nodded in understanding. "It's the very reason I sold my mother's house."

She remembered all too well, those early days after-

ward. It was very painful to be around a place that evoked
endless memories of her mother. Addison's heart ached
for Kellen. Dreyden wasn't just his brother but his best
friend, as well.

He sat on the rug opposite her, his back against a wing-
back armchair, his legs stretched out in front of him. His
legs looked so long and strong, the muscles of his thighs
discernible beneath the soft denim of his jeans. At some
point he'd taken his shoes off and his socked feet were
crossed at the ankles.

Addison cleared her throat, even though she had no
idea what she was about to say. Before she could speak
up, his phone rang.

"Sorry. It's probably one of my brothers. They have
been calling all day to check on me." He reached out to
grab the handset from the end table. "Hello."

The coldness in his voice, the abrupt change in his de-
meanor—Addison knew the call was regarding Dreyden.

"I'm sorry to have to tell you this way, but Dreyden
passed away recently." His gaze traveled to where she sat.

She gave him a reassuring smile.

Something flickered across Kellen's face.

"Sorry about that," he said, hanging up the phone. "It
was a friend of Dreyden's. She has been in Hong Kong
for the past year. She didn't know that he'd passed away.
She didn't take it very well."

"Sounds like she really cared for your brother."

"I think she did."

She eased down to the floor beside him. "I wish I could
make your pain go away."

"I would give anything to have my brother back with
me."

Addison embraced him.

Kellen held on to her as if holding on for dear life.

A delicious shudder heated her body at his touch. She closed her eyes and concentrated on keeping her breathing even. The warmth of his body captivated her. Addison felt the heat of desire wash over her like waves.

He smelled good, like warm skin and amber and spices, and his shoulder felt very solid beneath her hand. She let her hand drop to her side.

Kellen's hand reached out to catch it before she could withdraw.

Her eyes traveled to his lips. She wanted so much to feel the touch of his mouth against hers.

Where had that thought come from?

She knew the answer to the question, although she wasn't ready to acknowledge it.

Surprisingly, Kellen wasn't really thinking of her skin in a sexual sense, but more of the gentle give-and-take of shared heat. It was refreshingly simple and nice. Like a handful of summer sun on a dark winter's day.

However, the warmth building in the pit of his stomach coupled with the way she felt in his arms ignited something more.

Their gazes locked as his fingers wove with hers. For a long beat they simply stared at each other.

"Addison Evans," he said, so softly it was barely more than a whisper.

Then he leaned forward and pressed his lips to hers.

The world stood still.

His heart stuttered in his chest.

He forgot to breathe.

Then his mouth moved against hers once more and heat exploded in his belly. In that fraction of a second Kellen knew how it would be between them—passionate.

Addison jerked backward.

"Are you okay?" Kellen asked, reaching out to her.

She couldn't seem to look him in the eye, could barely force herself to lift her gaze to the middle of his chest. "Yes. Fine, thanks. All good."

He eyed her intently. "I don't want you to leave."

Kellen was drawn to her, in every possible way, and he knew, in his gut, that he was in no fit state to handle the intensity of his own feelings. They were too overwhelming, too confronting, when he was grieving the loss of his brother.

Yet his hunger for her would not be denied.

Kellen was a wonderful lover, powerful and intuitive and generous. He made her feel beautiful and sexy and happy and wild, but the reality was that she shouldn't have slept with him. She never should have let things progress to that point.

Don't. Don't do this to yourself.

Addison tried to reason that it was just sex. That it didn't matter.

Except that it did.

Something had happened when they were skin to skin. Something intense.

At least, it had been intense for her. Intense and tender and mind-blowing—all at once. Not what she'd expected, by a long shot. Not what she'd been looking for, either, but it had happened.

For her, anyway.

It had been a night for revelations, apparently.

But today was a different day. What took place between her and Kellen was now in the past, and she was determined to let it stay there.

She pulled into her parking space and turned off her car. Addison glanced around, looking to see if Kellen had already arrived.

Addison let out a sigh when she spotted his vehicle.

Inside the building, the elevator doors were beginning to shut, but she picked up her pace and slid inside just before they closed.

"Good morning," Kellen greeted.

"Good morning," she said in response. The last place she wanted to be was in such a small space with him.

Tension bounced off the walls, making the space feel especially tiny.

"I had a great time last night," Kellen began.

She interrupted him by saying, "What happened last night…it was a huge mistake."

"What do you mean it was a mistake?" he asked, confusion written all over his face. "It was something we both wanted."

"I'm a big girl with better sense than this. I should have stopped myself. Obviously." Addison drew a slow breath and pressed the heels of her hands against the dull throb at her temples. "Kellen, it never should have happened. I allowed my emotions to cloud my judgment."

He straightened up and stared at her. "I don't share your feelings, Addison. I don't regret what happened between us."

Addison met his gaze. "I didn't say I regretted what happened. I'm just saying that it was wrong."

"I still don't agree," Kellen uttered. "Everything about making love to you is right. You just don't want to admit it." He stared at her for a long beat, a muscle in his jaw flickering as though he was working to contain strong emotion. "Last night meant something to me, Addison. I want you to know that." His voice was all gravel and bass.

He reached for her but Addison retreated out of his grasp. "No, it can't happen again."

"Addison…"

She shook her head. "I've worked too hard for everything I have and I won't let a workplace romance destroy my efforts. Kellen, I'm sorry."

"Your career won't keep you warm on cold nights."

Addison didn't respond.

When the elevator doors opened, she rushed out, walking briskly to her office.

Chapter 15

Kellen couldn't believe that he had completely misread Addison. After the way they had made love, he assumed that they were building something together, but obviously he'd been wrong. He was preciously close to being completely in love with her, but it was obvious she didn't feel the same way.

When her gaze finally met his, he saw a distance in her eyes that broke his heart, a distance that made him feel like something had finished before it had ever really had a chance to begin.

He walked toward the elevator and pressed the button. Kellen was in need of some fresh air.

When he returned, he found Addison waiting on him in his office.

"What can I help you with?" Kellen asked.

"I wanted to make sure that I didn't sound harsh when we talked earlier."

He shook his head. "You didn't. We're fine."

"I know that you're grieving—"

"Addison, I heard you loud and clear," he said, interrupting her. "We're friends, and that's all we'll ever be. I understand completely, and I'm okay with it. Now if you'll excuse me, I have some work to do."

Kellen walked past her and around his desk. He sat down and turned on his monitor.

When he finally looked up, Addison was gone.

Addison stayed in the safety of her office. She wasn't ready for another face-to-face with Kellen. She was furious with herself for letting herself get so carried away with him. She knew better, even if Kellen did not consider it an issue.

Despite her resolve to keep her distance from him, Addison's body still craved his touch. She was relieved that Kellen hadn't tried to approach her. The only subjects she wanted to discuss with him were all work-related topics.

She had run into him a couple of times earlier. Once on the elevator and then when Addison was leaving for lunch. He barely spoke to her, which bothered her some, but it was for the best. There was no point in her getting upset when it was she who had set the terms.

Kellen was still grieving, too. He was still trying to make sense of his brother's death. Deep down, Addison wanted to be there for him but thought it best to stay out of his life. Her feelings for him were much too intense.

She pushed away from her desk and rose to her feet.

Addison walked over to the leather couch in her office and sat down. She thumbed through a stack of renderings, forcing her mind back on work.

It wasn't working, however.

Kellen weighed heavy in her thoughts.

A couple of hours later, Addison decided to leave for the day. She figured she could get more work done from home.

Addison left quickly, hoping to leave the building without running into Kellen. She didn't want him to know how strong of a hold he had on her.

She was not so lucky.

Kellen was waiting on the elevator when she turned the corner.

"Going home?" he asked.

Addison nodded. "I decided to work remotely for the rest of the day."

"I'll be here late tonight," Kellen stated. "Charles called a team meeting this afternoon."

"Do you need more time on the Haynes project?"

He shook his head. "I'm fine. I'll have it completed on time."

She missed their banter and easy conversations. Kellen was all business whenever he talked to her. They didn't even discuss football anymore. Addison told herself that she shouldn't expect anything different from him. He wanted more than she was willing to give him.

He no longer wanted anything to do with her. She couldn't deny that it hurt deeply, but she could not have it both ways.

Six weeks later, Addison sat inside the examination room, her arms folded across her chest. She had put off this appointment for as long as she could since missing her period. The past couple of weeks of nausea, exhaustion and hormones gone wild, prompted a call to the doctor's office. Her menstrual cycle was late and Addison needed confirmation of her suspicions.

Chewing on her bottom lip, she glanced around the room while wishing she were anyplace but here. Addison hated doctor visits but this one was unavoidable. Her eyes strayed to the door, silently willing someone to come tell her whatever.

"C'mon…" she muttered impatiently.

"Miss Evans," the doctor said as she entered the room, closing the door behind her. "We have your test results back."

"And?" Addison prompted.

"You're going to have a baby."

"Are you sure, Dr. Rivers?"

The one night she shared with Kellen would never be easily forgotten now that she was carrying his child.

"I can't believe this," Addison murmured. "I'm really pregnant."

"I gather this wasn't planned," Dr. Rivers said.

"It wasn't," she confirmed. "We were safe, so I'm in total shock by this."

After the appointment, she decided to go back to work. Addison needed to stay busy so that she didn't overthink her situation.

Stress churned in her stomach and tightened bands of steel around her head. Her hands were clammy. She probably shouldn't even be driving, given her current state of mind.

Fifteen minutes later, she locked the car with shaking hands.

Addison stared at the unobtrusive office doorway in front of her. A pot of cheerful geraniums tucked against the brick building soaked up the sun. She took a deep breath and walked inside, through the lobby and into a waiting elevator.

Just as she stepped out on the sixth floor, nausea roiled through Addison, tightening her stomach and making her mouth water. She gripped the doorframe. Any second now she was going to either throw up or pass out. When Addison felt stronger, she slowly made her way around her desk and sank down in her chair.

"Hey, are you okay?" Kellen asked as he strode toward

her desk. He wasn't sure, but he thought he'd glimpsed a flash of fear in her eyes.

"Yeah," Addison responded as casually as she could manage. "I'm fine. Why do you ask?"

"Tiffany said that you had a doctor's appointment this morning. I just wanted to see how you were doing." He hoped that she hadn't received any bad news. Kellen was still dealing with his brother's death. He couldn't bear the thought of losing someone else he cared about, even if that someone did not return his feelings.

She must have sensed his unease because she said, "Kellen, it was just a normal visit."

"Oh…okay," he uttered. "I was worried because you look like you hadn't been feeling well the past couple of days."

Addison hid her trembling fingers in the folds of her skirt. "Why do you say that?"

"You just haven't seemed like yourself."

"Hmm…well, there's nothing to worry about. According to my doctor, I'm in great health, Kellen."

Her stomach roiled again. She swallowed hard.

Relieved, he smiled. "I'm glad to hear it."

Addison wanted to take the conversation in another direction, so she asked, "Do you need something?"

"No, I was concerned about you, but now that I know that you're okay, I'm about to run out and grab some lunch. Do you want me to bring something back for you?"

"Where are you going?" she asked.

"To the deli on the corner. I'm in the mood for a Philly cheesesteak."

The thought of the greasy sandwich made her look as if she were about to be sick.

Addison shook her head. "I think I'll pass."

"Are you sure you're okay?" Kellen asked, concerned.

Addison nodded. "I'm just not in the mood for the deli today."

He eyed her for a moment before turning to leave. "Call me if you change your mind or want me to pick up something else for you."

"I appreciate the offer, but don't worry about me. I'll probably go out and get something to eat later today."

Addison released a soft sigh of relief when he left her office. She wasn't ready for Kellen to find out her secret. Truth be told, she wasn't sure that she ever wanted him to find out.

I'm pregnant. I'm going to be a mom.

Until today, she had not considered the idea of having children at this point in her life and career. Addison had always been more focused on her career path than settling down with a family.

She's keeping something from me, Kellen thought to himself when he left Addison's office. He rationalized that she was simply reluctant to discuss her health with her employee. He could understand why—it was her personal business.

She's okay. I don't need to worry about Addison. She's made it absolutely clear that she doesn't want me in her life.

In his office, Kellen focused his attention on a current project. Working helped to keep his mind off his grief.

Everyone in the family was still having a hard time dealing with Dreyden's death—only they avoided talking about it. Especially his parents. They were trying to be so strong for their children. What had happened was something so tragic that his family was forever changed.

It certainly changed Kellen's view on the world. He resolved never to take life for granted. He vowed to live in a way which would have made Dreyden proud.

Since losing his brother, Kellen felt a certain restlessness in his spirit. He felt alone and realized that he wanted a special someone to spend time with—that someone was Addison. He had strong feelings for her, and Kellen believed that she felt the same way about him, deep down. She was just too afraid to admit it.

He wasn't worried about what his coworkers thought, but it mattered greatly to Addison. She had yet to learn that she could go by the book when it came to work, but the heart…this was something entirely different.

Kellen had no desire to force her into admitting her true feelings. He would give her the space she needed, but in time she would come to him. She would not be able to put aside her feelings forever.

He longed to hold her in his arms once more. Addison had given him a glimpse into her heart the night they made love.

We belong together.

Kellen wasn't normally a patient man, but she was important to him and most of all—Addison was worth waiting for.

Chapter 16

"Girl, you look like you're putting on some weight," Tia said when Addison joined her in a booth near the window. "It looks good on you."

"Actually, that's why I wanted to have lunch with you today," she said as she took a seat. "I need to tell you something."

"What's up?"

"There's something you need to know." Addison paused for a heartbeat before announcing, "I'm pregnant, Tia."

"*What?* Are you serious?"

Addison nodded. "I'm still in shock myself."

"Girl, you need to tell me the scoop," Tia uttered. "I didn't even know you were dating someone. I thought we were besties."

"We are," Addison said. "You know that you are my dearest friend. Actually, you mean much more than that. You're like a sister to me."

"So why haven't you told me about this guy in your life?"

"Because it's not what you think, Tia."

"What do you mean?"

"I'm glad you're sitting down for what I'm about to tell you," Addison stated. "The father of my baby is Kellen Alexander. After his brother died, he was going through so much and I reached out to him. One thing led to another and we ended up in bed—it only happened once and we used protection..."

"Once is definitely all it takes," Tia murmured. "Wow...I certainly wasn't expecting all this." She glanced over her shoulder. "I need a glass of wine."

Addison released a soft sigh. "I could use a glass myself, but I can't have any."

"Have you decided what you're going to do? Does Kellen even know that you're pregnant?"

"I haven't said anything to him yet," she confessed. "I'm still trying to get used to the idea myself. As for what I'm going to do...I really don't know."

"Do you want this baby, Addison?"

"I have to be honest, Tia. I'm still too numb. I don't know how I feel, really. It's why I haven't made any major decisions one way or the other."

"It's probably wise not to do so. But whatever you decide, Kellen needs to know about the baby."

Addison agreed. "I know that you're right. I just don't know when or how I'm going to tell him something like this. It is so unexpected."

"You have to tell him."

"I know, but I want to wait until the time is right."

"When will that be, Addison? If you keep waiting— the baby will be here."

"It's not like we are in a relationship, Tia," Addison

stated. "It was a one-night stand. What are my other employees going to think when they find out?"

"You and Kellen are attracted to one another. I could see it so I'm sure your staff already has an idea of your feelings and probably won't be surprised."

"I still can't believe this," Addison uttered. "I'm going to be a mother."

Tia smiled. "Yes, you are."

"The thing is…I'm not so sure that I'm ready for this… for a baby."

"Are you thinking of terminating the pregnancy?" Tia asked in a low voice.

"To be honest, I'm not sure what I'm thinking. This is a lot to handle right now. Seeing Kellen every day doesn't make it any easier. At this point in my life all I've been thinking about is my career. A baby really doesn't fit into the picture I've painted for myself."

"I guess you and Kellen have a lot to discuss."

Addison nodded. "But first I have to decide if I'm ready to be a mom."

"It's your body, but I can't see you choosing to terminate your pregnancy."

"Tia, I know you don't believe in abortion."

"I'm not judging you, Addison," she interjected. "I'll support you regardless of what you decide to do."

"I have to be honest. The thought of terminating the pregnancy doesn't sit right with me, but there is always another option…adoption."

"I can't see you doing that, either," Tia stated. "And I'm pretty sure that Kellen will not agree to let some stranger raise his child."

"You're assuming that he will want to be a father. Trust me, Kellen isn't the type to settle down and raise a family."

* * *

"It's not like you to be so distracted," Kellen commented after the weekly team meeting.

Addison spared him a glance. "I'm sorry. I have a lot on my mind."

"What's going on with you?" he asked. "Addison, you haven't been yourself for a couple of weeks now."

"I have a lot on my mind."

"Do you want to talk about it?" Kellen inquired. "You were there for me when I was dealing with Dreyden's cancer and his passing. Let me return the favor."

She shook her head. "I'm really not ready to discuss anything. I hope you understand."

"I do," Kellen responded. "I want you to know that I'm here, and I'm also a good listener."

Addison gave him a smile. "Thank you for caring. I appreciate your concern."

"I know you think I'm throwing you a line but I'm not," he stated. "I really do care about you, Addison."

She met his gaze straight on. "Kellen, please don't confuse lust with real feelings. We shared one night together, but let's be realistic. You are not the type of man who is ready for a commitment."

"How do you know what kind of man I am?" he asked. "The truth is that you really haven't taken a chance to get to know me."

She leaned back in her chair and folded her hands across her chest. "So you're saying that you're ready to settle down."

"With the right woman," he responded truthfully. "I could go down that path."

Addison broke into a smile. "Kellen, you're a bachelor for life. I'm not sure you will ever find what you consider the *right* woman."

"How do you know that I'm not referring to you?"

he asked. "I think you're the one who's not interested in getting married. You're so afraid of your feelings for me that we can't even have a friendship."

Kellen's words left her speechless, just as he intended.

"I don't mind being your friend," Addison responded after a moment.

"You're kidding me right now."

"No, I'm not. Kellen, I mean it. I want to be a friend to you."

"But nothing more."

"I'm five years older than you, and I'm your boss. None of this bothers you, Kellen?"

"No, it doesn't," he responded with a shake of his head. "Age is nothing but a number. As for your being my boss, this will not always be the case. But for now, while I am in the office, I work for you. Outside—I expect you to be my woman."

Addison gathered up her notes. "I don't know why we're even having this discussion."

"Because I'm not going to give up on you."

On the way back to her office, Addison ran into Zaire Alexander in the hallway. The two had met at the Alexander Christmas party.

"You look beautiful," she told her. "Pregnancy certainly agrees with you."

"Thank you." Zaire placed a hand to her belly. "I was looking for my brother," she stated. "I was in the area so I thought I'd surprise him with a visit and take him to lunch."

"He was in his office," Addison responded.

"I checked, but he wasn't in there."

"Zaire, what are you doing here?" Kellen asked from behind Addison.

"I came to see you, silly."

He laughed.

"It was nice to see you again, Zaire," Addison said. "Congratulations on the upcoming birth of your baby."

"Is Addison seeing someone?" Zaire inquired when they were in her car.

"Not that I know of," he responded. "Why do you ask?"

"She has a glow about her. Her face is fuller than the last time I saw her."

Kellen agreed. "She's gained some weight. I noticed it, but I thought it best not to point it out. She still looks great."

"If I didn't know any better, I'd say that Addison's pregnant."

Kellen's eyebrows rose in surprise. *"P-pregnant?"*

Zaire nodded. "I could be wrong. It just may be weight gain. Maybe she didn't like being so thin."

He did not respond. Kellen's thoughts traveled back over the past few weeks and how strange Addison had been acting. He had also noticed her changing shape and the thickening of her waist. A pregnancy would certainly explain everything.

As soon as he returned to the office, Kellen intended to confront Addison with his suspicions. He had to know if she was pregnant with his baby. It bothered him to even think of her being with another man.

Chapter 17

"How was lunch with your sister?" Addison asked when Kellen entered her office. She had just returned from lunch with a coworker minutes before.

"Actually, it was very enlightening."

She glanced up at him briefly from her desk, and then turned her attention back to her computer screen. "Really? In what way?"

"Ever since I heard you saw a doctor, I've been worried about you."

"There was no need for you to worry. I'm okay. Doing well."

"I'm not sure I agree with you," Kellen said quietly as he closed the door to give them some privacy. "I have a suspicion that I know what's going on with you."

He suddenly had Addison's full attention. Surely he didn't know about the baby. There was no way that he could know. Stiffening in her chair, she uttered, "I'm not sure I know what you mean."

"Addison, look at me. I need you to be honest with me," Kellen stated. "Are you pregnant?"

A wave of apprehension flowed through her belly, causing her to grip the arms of her chair tightly.

"Addison," he prompted.

She nodded after a moment of tense silence.

"Is this my baby?" Kellen wanted to know.

"Yes," Addison responded tersely. She made it obvious that she was offended by his question, but he offered no apologies—she didn't really expect any.

"Why didn't you tell me?" he demanded. "Don't you think I have a right to know that I'm about to become a father?"

"I had every intention of telling you, but I needed some time to get used to the idea myself," she responded in a low voice.

Kellen suddenly broke into a grin. "Wow. I'm going to be a father."

His response surprised her. *"You're actually happy about this?"*

"Aren't you?" Kellen tugged up her chin so that he could see Addison's face. She looked away as if she wanted to hide. To be sure that her emotions were not painted there for him to see.

"The truth is that I'm not sure that I'm ready to be a mother." There, she'd said it. Addison stole a peek at Kellen, whose grin had disappeared as quickly as it had come.

He frowned. "I hope that you're not thinking of getting rid of my child—I won't allow it."

Addison met his gaze. "One thing you need to realize is that you don't have any control over my body, Kellen. It's my choice."

"I want my child." His tone brooked no argument.

She needed to make him aware of her feelings so she

said, "I have to be honest with you, Kellen. I have my career to think about. Motherhood is just not in my plan right now."

He looked at Addison as if seeing her for the first time. "Are you really that selfish?"

She bit back her irritation at his question. "We used precautions, Kellen. This baby… I never should've gotten pregnant."

"But you did," he argued. "That should tell you something. This child is a beautiful gift from God. The Lord allowed my brother to die but look what He's given us in return. I want my child and I'm prepared to raise him or her alone, if that's what I have to do."

Addison met his gaze. "Why is this child so important to you?"

"Because he or she is a part of me."

"This baby can't replace your brother, Kellen."

"I know that," he responded. "I'm not trying to replace Dreyden. I'm trying to take responsibility for the life we conceived."

"I need you to understand that this has been a complete shock to me, and that I need some time to think about my options."

"The only option should be how we are going to raise this baby."

"I don't need to feel pressured, Kellen."

"I'm not trying to pressure you, sweetheart. I'm just saying that I don't want you to terminate this pregnancy. It may have been ill-timed, but I already love this baby.

"Please don't take this child…my child away from me."

She dropped into the chair and rubbed at shoulder muscles gone as tight as cheap shoes. "Kellen, you don't really know me. How can you be so sure that I'll be a good mother?"

He studied her for a long, serious moment, then smiled. Addison's breath caught in her throat.

Kellen Alexander was devastatingly handsome when he smiled. "The eyes are the windows to the soul. That's what my mom used to say."

"Oh, so my eyes tell you that I'm good with children?"

He came toward her, hunkering down in front of the chair. "They tell me that you're scared right now, and that you're confused about this pregnancy. But you don't have to deal with this alone."

"Kellen, I…"

"Addison, I want you to marry me." He blurted out a laugh of surprise. "That wasn't how I planned to say it, but there you go."

Addison's mouth dropped open, and her eyes narrowed suspiciously. She couldn't believe that he had just uttered the words that he wanted to marry her.

What on earth is he thinking?

"Did you hear what I just said?" he asked.

Addison gave a slight nod. "I…I'm having some trouble believing that I heard you correctly."

"There's no confusion. You're having my baby, and I want to marry you."

She didn't get it. It didn't make sense.

"You don't know me," she began with a slow shake of her head. "Even if I'd talked your ear off from the minute we met until my little pilgrimage to the porcelain god… you couldn't really know me. My beliefs, my hang-ups, my shortcomings."

Kellen heaved a sigh and met her eyes.

She realized he was completely serious. Kellen was proposing to her in the middle of her office at two-thirty in the afternoon.

"You're not going to make this easy, are you?" he inquired. "Addison, you know that I'm crazy about you."

Addison felt his eyes on her but refused to meet his gaze. A woman could lose herself in those gray eyes of his and find herself agreeing to all kinds of madness.

The very idea of marrying Kellen Alexander was truly insanity in itself.

"I know that marriage is all about love, commitment and happily ever after. Addison, I actually want that for myself."

His cheekbones softened as he looked away. "I want a wife who loves me as much as I love her, and children of our own. I want what my parents have, what my siblings have—a relationship with someone where you're stronger together than being apart."

Addison had no idea that such a devastatingly sexy man could have such traditional values. It was a rare quality.

"Please say something," he uttered.

"I don't know what you want me to say, Kellen. This is all happening much too fast. We made love one night— this wasn't some relationship."

"It's only because you didn't want one, Addison. I've made it clear on more than one occasion that I want to be with you. Will you at least think about it?"

"I can't make any promises," Addison responded. "I'm sorry, but I can't do this right now. I need to focus on work so can we please table this discussion for now?"

"Sure, but we have to find time to finish this conversation."

She gave a slight nod. "I know. I just need a couple of days. This is a lot to handle and I have to prepare for a presentation tomorrow."

Addison lowered her gaze to the computer monitor, her stomach churning in trepidation. It did not ease her mind that her future and that of her child hung on her decision.

* * *

What was the matter with women these days?

Kellen had imagined that most women were naturally supposed to want babies. They seemed to constantly worry about their ticking biological clocks—especially the ones he had come into contact with.

He sighed heavily as he recalled Addison's reaction over her pregnancy. Just because his mother and sisters were nurturers didn't mean that Addison felt the same. Since the moment she had admitted being pregnant, his child had become his sole focus in life.

He was going to be a father.

Kellen was thrilled at the idea because he loved children and wanted some of his own—although he hadn't planned on it happening for a few years from now. It made sense to be with Addison. He cared for her a great deal. He wanted her. She dominated his thoughts day and night.

Kellen was in his office, a sheet of architect's renderings spread out on a wooden table. Wearing dark slacks and a long-sleeve oxford shirt with the sleeves rolled up, he looked casual but professional. Addison forced herself to walk toward him and perch a hip on one of the chairs that flanked his desk.

Kellen tapped a corner of the paper with a pencil. "Well, what do you think?"

He turned the sheet around so that she could see it.

Addison studied it. "It's beautiful, of course."

"But?"

"But what?" She sighed. "I'd flip these two wings." She pointed to a section of the blueprints.

Kellen nodded, his sharp gaze already assessing, dissecting.

"What else?"

"It would be nice to have a portico over the front entrance, so that on rainy days guests can get out of the car and stay dry. These are just suggestions and not commandments, Kellen."

"I like where this is going, Addison."

They studied the plans for another half hour, Kellen firing insightful questions at her, and Addison offering suggestions based on her experience.

But suddenly, they both fell silent.

Even in the midst of a business discussion, she was far too aware of him. But it was not like they could avoid one another. He was the father of her child, and they worked together. Addison could not let their personal lives become entwined with the jobs they had to do.

"I trust you with this," she told Kellen. "I have a conference call scheduled so I'll get out of your hair."

He nodded.

Addison walked the short distance to her office. She hadn't really expected him to just let her leave so easily. But then he was focused on his project. She tried to imagine him as a father but couldn't. He was just starting out with his career—she worried that a child could interfere.

She half listened to the conversation on the conference call; her mind was plagued with thoughts of Kellen. Addison was glad that it was being recorded. She would order a copy of the transcript later.

An hour later she sat at her desk completely immersed in her work. Addison was in her zone. Before she knew it, time had flown by and it was time for her to go home. She packed up her laptop and prepared to leave. As Addison neared Kellen's office, she could not resist sticking her head inside. "I just stopped by to say good-night."

He looked up from his computer monitor, meeting her gaze. "I'm glad to see that you're leaving earlier than usual. You need your rest."

She walked inside the office. "Hey, I don't need you

to start trying to babysit me. I'm more than capable of taking care of myself."

"I know that, Addison," Kellen responded. "But you shouldn't have to—I'm here and I want us to be a team. We're in this together. Why are you trying to do this alone?"

She switched her tote from one shoulder to the other. "I'm just used to having to take care of myself."

"You're not alone anymore, sweetheart." He paused a moment before saying, "Addison, I'd like you to do something for me."

"What?" she asked.

"Join me on Sunday for dinner with my family."

Puzzled, she asked, "Why do you want me there?"

"I want you to get to know us better," Kellen responded. "I would assume that you'd want this, too. I'd like for my family to get to know you better, as well."

"I would like to get to know your family more," she admitted. "So the answer is yes."

He smiled. "Great."

"I'll see you tomorrow." Addison stifled a yawn. "I need to get out of here. Don't work too late."

Smiling, Kellen returned his attention to his monitor.

"Kellen, why did you really want me to come here?" Addison inquired. "I was thinking about this on the way here. I'm sure it's not just because you want me to get to know your family better. What's really going on?"

"I want you here."

"Which basically tells me nothing," she responded with a wry smile.

"Okay, the truth is that I want to celebrate our baby with my family."

"You told them?" Her voice rose in panic. She was afraid that his parents would find her completely un-

suitable for Kellen. Addison wasn't ready for that type of criticism to be heaped on her head. "Your mother is going to naturally think I'm a gold digger," she uttered. "Thanks a lot, Kellen."

Her temper was a work of art. First Addison's eyes flashed dark fire. Then they narrowed as if she was contemplating where she wanted to punch him.

"After losing Dreyden, I knew that they would welcome some good news. Sweetheart, your carrying my baby is great news to my family."

Bracing one hand on her car, Addison closed her eyes, willing away the sudden onset of nausea. When she spoke, her words were soft and accusing. "How could you do this to me, Kellen? This situation is awkward enough but you had to make it worse. Now your father knows that we slept together. You are one of my employees."

"He's not a prude, Addison. Besides, my dad already sensed our feelings for one another. Trust me, this doesn't surprise him."

She swallowed hard. "I can't believe that you would ambush me like this."

"It wasn't an ambush, Addison."

"There's no other word for it," she quickly interjected.

"Why are you so upset? They were going to find out, anyway."

"When I was ready, Kellen," she countered. "I'm still in my first trimester of this pregnancy. Anything could happen."

He stepped closer to Addison and laid a hand on her cheek. A few tendrils curled around her face and whispered against the feel of his hand. Her hair... Kellen resisted the temptation thus far to sink his hands into that rich carpet of darkness. It was out of her customary ponytail and trickled down her back. There wasn't a man in this hemisphere that could resist hair like that. "I'm sorry. I guess I didn't think this through." He made the apology clear.

Addison sighed, a mixture of frustration and resignation. "No, you didn't."

"Please come back inside."

She shook her head. "I can't face them right now. I can't believe you did this to me." She didn't want to answer the questions that she knew they all must have. Addison could only imagine what they must think of her. Malcolm had to be so disappointed.

She rushed off to her car and climbed inside.

She drove away before Kellen could stop her.

As Addison turned onto the long, winding road that led back to Los Angeles, she uttered a string of profanities under her breath when she glanced in the rearview mirror and saw a black Mercedes hurtling toward her in hot pursuit.

I can't believe he's actually following me.

Apparently, this was her day to be taken completely off guard.

Furious, Addison pulled to the side of the road, shut off the engine and stepped down from her Land Rover.

Kellen followed suit and met her more than halfway, his sheer presence forcing her to back up against her vehicle. Addison put her hands on her hips and glared at him. "What in the world do you think you're doing?"

He stood there like a rugged model from a high-end men's magazine, legs spread and arms crossed over his chest. His expensive suit fit him perfectly, drawing attention to his muscular thighs and broad shoulders.

"I can't let you leave like this. We need to talk." The words were quiet, his gaze sober, his face wiped clean of all expression.

"You ambushed me, and I don't like it."

"Why do you keep saying that?"

"You knew that I wasn't sure I wanted to keep the baby so you decided to tell your family." She gave a frustrated shake of her head. "How can you think of being a father when you still have so much growing up to do?"

"How can you be so cold and disinterested in your own child?" Kellen countered, his mouth tight with tension. "I know I haven't handled things well, but I think we can come to an understanding. Stop trying to make things difficult."

"I'm not," she shot back. "If you had just waited, I would've told you that I'd made a decision. I am keeping my child. I want this baby, but I'm not ready to shout it to the world."

Kellen released the breath he was holding.

"I need you to stop trying to manipulate me."

"I'm sorry."

"No, you're not," Addison responded. "You're willing to do whatever it takes to keep your child safe. Although I didn't like it, I can understand why you did what you did, Kellen. You want your child."

"We both want this child," he corrected. "Which means that I want to make our family complete, Addison."

For a moment Kellen stared at Addison, picturing her in a long, white dress, her mass of dark hair falling over her shoulders, and he couldn't breathe. "I want to marry you."

"I honestly never really figured you for the marrying kind."

"I didn't think so, either, until I met you," he responded. "I care a great deal for you, Addison. More than I've ever felt for any other woman."

"I...I don't really know what to say."

"You could say yes to my proposal."

Recovering from the shock, she said, "Technically, you

haven't proposed to me, but that's fine because I don't think that we are anywhere near the idea of marriage."

"Is it because you don't have feelings for me?"

Addison met his gaze as she responded, "You know that I feel something for you. It's way too soon to think about marriage, Kellen. That's all I'm saying."

"I want a family."

"I'm sorry, but I can't think about that right now."

"Addison, I can't stop thinking about you," he muttered.

Taking her shoulders in his big hands, Kellen drew her close and settled his mouth over hers in a gentle, drugging caress of warm, firm lips.

Long and slow and unabashedly intimate.

Kellen took charge as if he had every right to kiss her senseless.

Her body was warm, and standing beneath the unforgiving sun, it was no wonder.

"Put your arms around me," he said.

"I'm not going to marry you just because we're having a baby." But even as Addison whispered the words, her mental resistance to him crumbled in the wake of a tidal wave of longing. Addison buried her face in his shoulder as he stroked her hair.

She needed him.

Painfully.

Chapter 18

"What's going on in here?" Kellen inquired two days later. He had stopped by Addison's office to check on her.

"I'm going away for a couple of days," Addison announced as she packed up her laptop. "I'm taking my computer with me. It's just in case the team needs to send me any documents."

"Mind if I tag along?" he asked, half joking.

She zipped her tote closed, and then said, "Kellen, I really need some time alone. I have a lot to think about, and I can't do it here. I hope you understand."

His expression grew serious. "I do."

Addison headed toward the door with Kellen walking beside her.

"I'll only be gone for a couple of days. We can talk about everything when I get back."

"You haven't changed your mind about keeping the baby, have you?" he wanted to know.

Addison shook her head. "You can relax. I'm not going

away to get rid of the baby, Kellen. It's just that my life is going in a different direction, and I need to think about some stuff."

"I'm going to miss you."

She smiled. "I'm sure you have a busy weekend planned. The fundraiser for the center is on Saturday."

"Yeah, I was kind of hoping that you would be my date."

"I hate missing it—but if I went, I wouldn't be any fun. My mind is too preoccupied right now."

"I understand." Kellen stood in her path, blocking her escape. "I need to know. Am I the reason you're leaving?"

"Not really," she responded. "I mean...partly. I just can't think straight right now."

"I didn't mean to add any stress to your life."

"You didn't, Kellen. I'm just super emotional right now. I've been working a lot, and I think a few days away will do me good. Please promise me that you're not going to try and follow me."

"I give you my word." He pulled her close to him and kissed her on the lips. "I'll see you when you get back, then."

She gave him a tiny smile. "It's a date."

"I can't believe that you're actually thinking of settling down and having a family," Blaze whispered to Kellen, leaning forward. "I thought you were going to hang on to your singleness for a while longer." They sat outside on the balcony of Ari's condo.

He agreed. "That was the original plan, but things changed for me when Dreyden died. I just think differently now, especially with Addison having my baby."

"Do you love her or is this because she's carrying your child?"

"I do love her," Kellen confirmed. "I would still want

to marry her even if she weren't pregnant, Blaze." He grinned. "I've never met a woman like her."

Blaze signaled to Ari to join them.

"You need to hear this," he told him. "Kellen, tell him what you just told me."

Kellen laughed. "I know. I just lost my playa card permanently. I told Blaze that I really love Addison, and that I've never met anyone like her."

Ari busted into a grin.

"Hey, didn't Ryan tell us that men in excellent health were about 89 percent more likely to die if they were single compared to married men? I know that I gave you guys a hard time for your declarations of love and adoration, but now I know what you meant. Addison's changed my life."

"We're happy for you," Ari said. "We can certainly use some good news right about now."

Blaze and Kellen both agreed.

"Have you proposed to her yet?"

He nodded. "I just haven't convinced her to say yes, Ari. She is going away for a few days to think about everything."

"Does she love you?" asked Blaze.

"She does, but she won't admit it to herself," Kellen responded. "She is worried about how it would look to the rest of her employees. She's also bothered that she's five years older than me."

Ari shrugged in nonchalance. "Age doesn't matter."

"I told her that."

Blaze reached for his glass of wine. "Just be sure that Addison loves you as much as you seem to love her. I don't want to see you get hurt."

"I know that she loves me. It's in her eyes whenever she looks at me."

"Do you know where she's going?"

Kellen shook his head. "She wouldn't tell me. Addison knew I'd follow her there. She made me give her my word that I'd give her some space."

Chapter 19

Addison didn't leave until early the next morning.

The lane was long and straight, unpaved, leading to a beachfront, two-story house in Malibu with white siding and black shutters. Addison stared at it, impressed with the amount of work Tia and her husband had put into this property. It had been a foreclosure they discovered and fell in love with, so they decided to purchase the property and give it a complete overhaul.

She looked around. There were not any neighbors nearby. The land surrounding the house was spattered sparsely with palm trees.

Isolated.

Inside the house, Addison sat her leather weekender on the sofa.

The master bedroom was on the second level and large, with a double dresser, mirror and a sturdy pine bed. The coverlet was teal and lacy. Addison wasn't surprised at the choice in color because it was one of Tia's favorites.

The room was too pretty.

Too perfect, Addison thought as she put her bag on a chair beside the nightstand.

She took her clothes out and put them in the dresser.

A cosmetic bag held toiletries—soap, shampoo, toothbrush, deodorant. Those she took to the bathroom.

She didn't allow her thoughts to take over until she had unpacked. Addison sat down on the edge of the bed.

I'm pregnant, and I'm keeping the baby. What does this mean for my career?

Kellen says that he wants to marry me. I don't want to get married just because I'm pregnant. I do have feelings for him, though.

The flat-screen TV held little interest and the book she'd brought with her had hit a dull spot.

She sat on the porch, watching the ocean. Addison had no idea how long she sat out there, but she didn't move to go inside until her stomach started making low, guttural noises.

She had a salad for dinner.

Addison was in bed before ten o'clock.

Saturday morning, Addison was up early and back on the porch. Huge cumulus clouds bobbed along in a sea of blue as the sun rose higher and the day began to get hot.

Hours later she sat curled up on the couch with her book, but Addison was having trouble keeping her mind on the story line. She tried to go back to her book, but her mind kept wandering. She found herself looking out the window and down the length of sandy beach.

The late-summer air seemed to be holding its breath, waiting for something. She felt that same sense of anticipation inside her like the flutter of butterfly wings. A strange feeling came over Addison. Something was about to happen.

Addison got up to get a bottle of water when she felt a sharp pain, which caused her to double over.

She sat back down. It was too soon to feel the baby kicking. Addison had read in one of the pregnancy books that it wasn't uncommon to experience aches and pains. She swallowed her fear and decided to stay put for a while.

Addison went from calm to panic in a matter of minutes when she realized that she was spotting. She reached for her phone and pressed 9-1-1.

"I'm pregnant. Please don't let me lose my baby," she cried when the paramedics reached her.

They wasted no time in getting her to the hospital.

While she waited to be seen by a doctor, Addison picked up her cell phone.

She was scared, and she didn't want to go through this alone.

She needed Kellen.

"How are you and the baby?" he asked after rushing into her hospital room. Kellen left the fundraiser as soon as he received Addison's call and heard the panic in her voice. He hadn't prayed since Dreyden's death until after he hung up the phone with her.

Addison's fingers shook a little as she stared into Kellen's eyes. "I have never been so scared in my life." She reached for his hand. "I really thought I was losing the baby."

Kellen embraced her. "But the doctor said that everything was fine, right?"

"I never knew just how much I wanted our child until I started spotting." Addison glanced up at him, her eyes filled with unshed tears. "I already love this baby so much."

"What did the doctor say?"

"He told me that everything looks good and the baby's heartbeat is strong. They're going to keep me overnight, though."

Kellen covered her hand with his and squeezed. "I was really scared when you called me," he said softly.

"I'm so sorry for the things I said to you when you found out."

"Look at me, Addison," he commanded, when she dropped her eyes.

She met his gaze and was caught, unable to look away.

"You don't have to apologize for anything. I really need you to hear me. I'm not going anywhere," he told her. "I am staying right here with you and our baby."

She wiped away her tears with the back of her hand. "Thank you for coming."

"I'm glad you called me," Kellen responded. His arms stiffened around her, his fingers digging into her spine as he pulled her closer, tighter. As if he could wrap himself around her as a shield, keeping her safe.

Protected.

"You're safe with me," he vowed.

Addison never wanted to be anywhere else.

Realizing she'd plummeted into dangerous thinking, Addison drew in a little more of his calm, got her thoughts and her breathing under control then slowly pulled back. "I'm sorry for crying all over you like that," she said, wrinkling her nose in embarrassment. "I don't usually break down like that."

"It's fine," Kellen told her. "No one can be strong all of the time, sweetheart. We're just not made that way."

"I really hated interrupting your fundraiser."

"I was bored," he commented with a chuckle. "I didn't mind leaving. Addison, I want you to know that I promise to provide for you and our baby. I promise that I won't be the one to hurt you."

Her eyes filled with shimmering, unshed tears at his words. Kellen meant them. That, she didn't doubt.

And for her they were more romantic than any flowery vows from a book could ever be. "I believe you," she murmured.

"My mother wanted to come with me, but I promised to call her with an update. In fact, I need to call her now." Kellen pulled out his cell phone.

"Mom says hello," he said when he ended the call a short time later.

"Hello back," she murmured with a smile.

"My parents are excited about our baby."

Addison started to cry again.

Kellen folded his arms around her, pulling her close to his chest. She remained locked in on herself, arms banded around the pillow. He tucked her head beneath his chin and waited her out. After what felt like a long time, her body softened and her head rested more heavily on his shoulder.

"I'm so tired," she said, and he knew she was talking about more than physical tiredness.

"You'll be okay, Addison. The baby is fine. Everything is going to be okay."

Her breathing evened out.

After a few more minutes she stirred in his arms, pushing away from his chest. She glanced at his face briefly before grabbing more tissues.

The glimpse was enough for him to see she was embarrassed now that the crisis had passed.

"I apologize for my meltdown."

"You don't have to apologize, sweetheart."

"Yeah, I do. I'm supposed to be a strong, independent woman. I'm supposed to be able to handle anything." Her voice sounded husky and thick.

"So you're saying that you aren't supposed to feel anything or be afraid? That's crap, Addison."

"I don't know," she responded. "Sometimes it doesn't feel like I can. Sometimes it feels as though if I stop, that'll be it. I'll be locked in one place—never getting better, never moving forward. That's not what I want for my life. I've worked so hard to be as good as or better than my male counterparts."

"Addison, you're really overthinking this too much. You're good at your job, so just relax."

"Being a woman in this industry is challenging enough, but when one aspires to get into senior management—it's not easy."

"I don't want you thinking about this right now." He kissed away the beginnings of what he assumed was her protest. "Tell me, are we having a girl or a boy?"

"I don't know," she responded with a smile. "The doctor ordered a sonogram, but I think it's much too soon to know the sex."

"I'm hoping for a little girl," he told her.

Addison broke into a grin. "Me, too."

Their conversation came to a halt when a nurse entered the room to check the fetal monitor.

"I need to go to the bathroom," she announced when they were alone again in the room.

Kellen was instantly by her side as she swung her legs off the bed. "Let me help you."

"Just pull that wheelchair over here. I'll be right back," Addison said as she pulled herself out of the bed and into the wheelchair. The seat of the chair felt particularly cold against her bottom as she reached down and grabbed her robe from the edge of the bed, and then wheeled herself into the bathroom.

Once there she freshened up, noting her reflection in the mirror that hung on the wall over the sink. *I look so pale.*

Kellen was about to knock when she opened the door.

"I was getting worried."

"I'm fine."

He rolled the wheelchair over to the bed and assisted her back in it.

Kellen looked at her and found her staring at him, a smile on her face. "What?"

"You never cease to amaze me," she murmured. "You are very protective of those you care about."

He nodded. "A family is stronger together."

Addison reached over and took his hand in her own. "You really are a very special man."

Grinning, Kellen replied, "I've been trying to tell you that from the first day we met."

She laughed.

He kissed her hand. "You're very special to me, too."

Addison yawned.

"Why don't you try and get some sleep, sweetheart?"

"You're not leaving, are you?"

Kellen shook his head. "I'll be right here unless they kick me out of here."

"I don't want you to leave," she said.

He knew it was not easy for Addison to ask him to stay. Kellen could tell that she hated feeling what she considered weak and needy.

"I'll be here," he promised.

Kellen had no intention of leaving that hospital, even if it meant he had to sleep in the waiting area. He wanted to stay close by in case Addison wanted or needed him.

The next day, Addison was released from the hospital shortly after twelve noon.

"I'm so ready to get out of here," she murmured. "I have never liked hospitals or the way that they smell. I spent a lot of time in them when my mother was sick."

"You know that the doctor placed you on bed rest for the next couple of days," Kellen stated. "I mean to honor his request, even if I have to tie you down."

She nodded. "You won't get an argument from me. I'm going to do exactly as he instructed. I won't risk anything happening to my baby and I certainly don't want to end up back in a hospital room."

"He doesn't want you to leave town until after your follow-up with him in three days."

"I know, and I'm fine with it. I would rather make sure everything is fine with the baby before I leave, as well."

A nurse entered the room with a wheelchair.

The only time Kellen left her side was to pull the car up to the entrance. He helped Addison inside and then drove to the beach house.

He insisted on carrying her into the house.

She was nearly weightless in his arms and so achingly fragile. "You are going straight to bed," Kellen told her. "I'm going to get us something to eat and while I'm gone I don't want you getting out of bed."

She nodded. "Can you stay with me for a little bit? I really missed you."

"If this is what you want," Kellen responded with a tender smile. "I missed you, too, but I know that you wanted time alone."

"All I did was think about how much I wanted to see your handsome face again. You were right all along. I really care about you, Kellen."

"You already know that I'm crazy about you," he responded. "I was so worried when I got your call last night." Kellen reached over and gave her hand a gentle squeeze. "I'm going to take care of you until you give birth to our child."

She gave him a sidelong glance. "What about afterward?"

"Hmm…"

Addison tossed a small, square pillow at him.

Kellen made sure Addison was settled in bed and sleeping before he left the house in search of a grocery store. He found one less than a mile away.

When he returned to the beach house, he found her still asleep. Kellen decided to have lunch ready by the time she awakened.

He walked back to the bedroom to check on her. His breath caught in his throat. She was so beautiful, and she looked peaceful lying there.

Addison stirred slightly.

Kellen walked back to the kitchen.

Twenty minutes later he heard her when she called out for him.

"Hey, beautiful…"

She sat up in bed, plumping pillows behind her. "How long was I asleep?"

"Almost two hours." He sat a cup on the granite-top nightstand. "It's herbal tea. No caffeine."

Picking up the lovely ivory cup scattered with blue forget-me-nots, she smiled and replied, "Thank you."

Kellen had prepared a tray of sandwiches, as well—tiny, slightly ragged squares of white bread with the crusts removed.

Peanut butter and honey.

A smile tugged at the corners of her mouth.

"I remembered you telling me that whenever you weren't feeling well, your mom made you these."

"This is so sweet of you, Kellen."

He breathed a sigh of relief that she was pleased. Making her happy was at the forefront of his mind.

Chapter 20

Addison picked up a piece of sandwich, chewed and swallowed. The familiar tastes from her childhood opened a floodgate of memories.

Kellen ate two of the mini-sandwiches and finished off a bottle of water.

For some reason Addison found herself infinitely fascinated by the play of muscles in his throat as he swallowed. Everything about Kellen was intensely virile and dangerously sexual, a reminder of how much of an effect he had on her.

He sat back in his chair and drummed his fingers on the arms. "I want you to get some rest when you finish eating, okay?"

"You *are* staying here with me, aren't you?" she asked. "I…I don't want to be alone."

Kellen knew she was afraid of something happening to the baby while she was here alone. He had no intentions of letting that happen. "Definitely," he responded. "I don't have a problem sleeping in one of the guest rooms."

"Thank you," she responded. "I'd feel much better knowing that you're here."

He rose to his feet and kissed her on the cheek. "I'm glad."

"Kellen, maybe you should sleep in here with me," Addison stated, meeting his eyes. "I really don't mind."

"Are you sure?" he questioned. "I want you to be comfortable."

She gave a nod. "Yes, I want you to stay with me."

He sat down on the bed beside her.

Addison took his hand in hers. "Kiss me."

When their lips met and her mouth moved beneath his, responding hesitantly, sleeping was the last thing on Kellen's mind. He groaned, deepening the kiss without conscious thought, plumbing the sweet depths of her mouth with his tongue.

She whimpered and pressed nearer, sending a rush of excitement like a tidal wave through his chest.

Addison snuggled against him as she stifled a yawn. She loved the feel of his nearness. For now this was just what she needed.

Addison tossed and turned for an hour, unable to sleep. She glanced over at Kellen, watching him as he slept. She didn't want to disturb him so she eased out of bed and walked to the windows, drawing the thick draperies aside and peering out into the dark. The late-night oceanfront scenery was serene.

She hugged her arms around her body and decided she had had enough as her limbs trembled with fatigue.

"What are you doing up?" Kellen asked in the darkness.

She turned, making out his body in the moonlit room.

He was sitting up in bed. "You should be resting, sweet-heart."

"I couldn't sleep. I think I slept too much earlier."

He crossed the room in quick strides and scooped her into his arms. "Well, read a book or something, but you must stay off your feet."

"You can't spend all your time carrying me around," she muttered. It was a token protest at best. His warmth surrounded her even as his strength filled her with an odd contentment.

"I'll carry you until you give birth to our child if I have to," Kellen said as he placed her in bed. He walked to the other side and climbed in beside her.

"I'm really glad that you're here."

"I wouldn't be anywhere else." He placed a kiss on her forehead. "You and our child need me."

"I never thought I'd say this, but you're right," Addison admitted. "I do need you. I don't think I can go through this pregnancy alone."

"I'm not going anywhere."

"Kellen, you feel so good," she breathed, her hands gripping his shoulders then sliding down the hard mus-cles to curve over the rock-hard roundness of his biceps. "So strong. Big. I feel safe with you."

He placed a gentle kiss on her forehead. "I'm glad be-cause I would never do anything to hurt you."

She yawned as sleepiness gradually began to over-take her.

"You should try and go back to sleep, sweetie," he murmured. "You need your rest."

After that she surrendered to the luring call of slumber.

Kellen awoke abruptly, his internal alarm clock set for 6:00 a.m. For a moment he was completely disoriented and confused because his surroundings were unfamiliar. Suddenly, everything came flooding back.

Though it was an anomaly to begin the day fully dressed in a woman's bed, he'd promised that nothing would happen between them. He knew that her pregnancy was still high risk. Kellen wasn't about to tempt fate because of his lust.

Addison and the baby were in crisis.

She sighed in her sleep and nestled more closely into his embrace.

He wanted her and this feeling between them. They shared a bond that could never be broken.

Kellen eased out of bed and walked barefoot into the living room. There was no doubt in his mind that Addison was the woman for him. He loved her completely. Despite their rocky relationship from the start, she had seared a path straight to his heart.

He could almost hear Dreyden laughing and teasing him about being in love. There were times that Kellen found it hard to believe. He still grieved for his brother; but in the midst of that grief, he had been given something so special—Addison and their unborn son or daughter.

With Addison, he was whole. She was heaven, pure and simple. She made him feel as if nothing could scare her, nothing could hurt her, as long as he was close.

Kellen had already made them both breakfast including blueberry muffins, a spinach-and-bacon omelet and smoothies.

"You made me breakfast?" Addison exclaimed. "Wow, I'm impressed. I had no idea that you could cook."

"I have many talents," Kellen responded with a grin.

"So I see."

"This is delicious," she murmured after sampling the omelet.

When they finished eating, she told him, "I want you

to know that I'm really grateful to you for coming to the hospital to be with me. I have never been so scared in my life."

"You don't have to keep thanking me," Kellen responded. "This is my child, and I don't want to be left out of anything that concerns him or her."

"I want you to know that you're spoiling me," Addison acknowledged. "I can get used to this."

He smiled. "I hope so because I intend on spoiling you forever."

She laughed. "You say that now."

"I mean it," Kellen stated. "I'm crazy about you, and all I want is to make you happy."

"It would make me happy to be able to sit on the porch. I'm feeling a little stir-crazy in this house and so close to the ocean."

"Just for a little while," he said.

Addison smiled. "Thank you."

Kellen carried her out to the front porch after she had pleaded for some fresh air and sunlight.

"You didn't have to carry me out here."

"You're supposed to be in bed, remember?"

"Hey, I'm just sitting out here. I promise I'll be good." Addison held up her book. "I'm going to do some reading."

"You don't mind if I take a swim, do you?"

She shook her head. "Have fun for me, too."

Addison shaded her eyes against the bright arcs of sunlight reflecting off the Pacific and interfering with her view of the gorgeous specimen of a man diving into the ocean. She actually envied the water as it slid over Kellen's rock-hard body.

She let the sight of his body, cutting strong and sure through the ocean waves, soothe her, relaxing away the tension and worries.

Chapter 21

Kellen didn't like the idea of Addison driving home but she refused to leave her car in Malibu. He followed her all the way home, which was not surprising at all. She had come to realize that this protective nature was a facet of his personality.

She liked it. Addison also liked that he didn't make her feel weak or any less independent. He knew when to give her space. Loving Kellen was easy, although she fought against it for months. It felt so natural and so right.

"I think you should get in bed." His words interrupted her thoughts.

She turned to look at him. "I feel fine."

"You still have to take it easy, sweetheart."

Addison kissed him. "Kellen, if it makes you more comfortable, I'll sit on the couch and not move until it's time for bed."

"I'll agree to that compromise."

"Ah." Addison couldn't help it. She laughed.

His lips twitched, but he didn't smile. Kellen gave her a serious, peering-all-the-way-into-her-soul kind of look, instead. As if he knew what was in her heart and was waiting for a confession.

"I need to tell you something."

"What is it?" Kellen asked.

"I love you. I love you so much that my heart hurts when you're not around."

He wrapped his arms around her. "You have no idea how long I've waited to hear you say those words. I love you, Addison, and I really want you to be my wife. Will you marry me?"

She looked up at him. "Yes, I'll marry you." Addison had opened the door to her emotional closet—that secret place where she put away all the feelings she had been too afraid to deal with—she was no longer scared. "I never really realized just how much I want a home. Someplace, someone that accepts me for who I am."

"I accept everything about you, Addison. I love you and I want to spend the rest of my life with you."

Smiling, she said, "I want the same thing. I tried so hard to fight my feelings for you, but it was useless."

"So I'm irresistible?"

Addison laughed. "And humble."

Kellen wrapped his arms around her. "We are going to have a good life together. This is my promise to you."

"You do know everyone in the office is going to be shocked by the news that we're getting married."

He shrugged in nonchalance. "I don't care what they think."

She surveyed his face. "You really mean it. I hope to get to that place in my life. What others think of me still does matter."

"Just remember that we are strong together as a family. You're going to be my wife, and I'll protect you with my life."

Addison grinned. "I caught the rhyming thing…"

He laughed. "I'm cool like that."

Later that evening Addison paused in the doorway of the kitchen, drinking in the sight of Kellen. He was wearing old, faded jeans and a light blue shirt with the sleeves rolled up. She forced herself to enter the room. "I'm starving. Thanks for putting this together."

He had found plates and glassware in the cupboard and sat them on the counter.

The spaghetti and garlic bread smelled delicious.

"Once you've had my spaghetti sauce," Kellen began, "You won't want anyone else's."

"Hmm…I don't know about that."

"Wait until you try it."

"My sauce is pretty good, Kellen."

"I see we're going to have a cook-off," he challenged.

He held out her chair.

Her throat tightened when she spotted the clear-glass vase in the center of her table. Kellen had somehow found the time to pick up a bouquet of roses. The gesture affected her deeply.

"Dig in," he said, taking his own seat.

He had poured her a tall glass of water, and wine for himself.

They ate in silence for several minutes.

Addison wiped her lips with a napkin and sat back in her seat, regarding him with suspicion.

"What?" Kellen questioned, looking innocent.

"This tastes exactly like my sauce."

He took a sip of wine. "Really? That's interesting."

"It sure is," Addison said, still eyeing him. "How did you get my recipe?"

"I saw your family cookbook. It said that it was your mother's recipe so I thought I'd make it for you."

She smiled. "You're so sweet."

"Surely, you're just not realizing this now."

"No, I've known it for a while."

After they finished their meal, they settled down in the living room

Her silence began to bother him.

"What's on your mind?" Kellen asked.

"We haven't known each other very long, and now I'm pregnant and we're talking about getting married. Do you ever wonder that we're moving too quickly?"

"No, not at all," he responded. Kellen had been expecting this argument, and he was prepared. "It doesn't take months or years to know that what we share is intense, special and forever."

"Have you ever been in love before?" Now that question was one Kellen hadn't expected.

"No," he admitted, "but this is why I recognize it now. I have no doubts about how I feel, Addison." Her laughter filled his heart with the music that had been missing from his life. He'd never known anyone like her before, a woman who was both incredibly vulnerable and yet possessed a steely strength and a need for independence.

Reaching into his pocket, Kellen pulled out a small, velvet box and flipped the lid.

"I love you. That's the honest truth. As far as I'm concerned, nothing else matters."

Taking her hand in his, Kellen slipped the platinum band with the huge, flawless stone onto the third finger of her left hand.

The seconds that elapsed as Addison ran her thumb around the ring felt like an eternity.

Finally, she raised her eyes to meet his. "Kiss me."

Kellen lowered his head, his lips searching for hers.

Addison's lashes fluttered and settled at half-mast, shielding her emotions as they kissed.

He pulled away from her slowly. "Do you have any doubts, sweetheart?"

Addison smiled up at him, utterly feminine, deliciously warm and appealing. "I never knew I could feel this way about anyone. I do love you, Kellen, and no, I don't have any doubts."

"I'm sorry I waited so long to come out here but it's been hard," Kellen said as he knelt down in front of his brother's grave. He placed a bouquet of flowers against the gravestone. "It was difficult for me to think of you lying here in an eternal sleep. You should be here in the world living out the rest of your life...."

He shook his head sadly. "The truth is that I really miss you, Dreyden, and I'm never going to be okay with this. I'm sorry, but it's not right that you had to die. I'm angry about your leaving. Ari and Blaze keep telling me that you're no longer in pain, and while I don't want you hurting all of the time, I still wish you were here among the living."

Kellen snatched up a weed. "One of the reasons I came is because I have some good news," he announced. "I'm getting married, and I'm going to be a father. Can you believe that?" He paused a moment as if waiting for a response. "I love Addison in a way that I've never loved another woman."

He chuckled softly. "I'm pretty sure that you're not surprised. You called it shortly after I started working with her. As usual, you were right, big bro. If I have a son, I'm going to name him after you. He will know all about his uncle Dreyden."

"I thought I'd find you here."

Kellen glanced over his shoulder to find Ari standing

nearby. "I came to tell Dreyden about the baby and my upcoming marriage."

Ari smiled. "I know that he would be very happy for you."

"I know." Kellen glanced up at his eldest sibling. "What are you doing out here?"

"I was actually looking for you," Ari responded. "I've been worried about you since we lost Dreyden."

"Aren't you angry over his death?"

Ari nodded. "I felt the same anger over April's death, as well."

Kellen recalled how grief stricken Ari had been when his first wife died. It had taken nearly two years for him to get over losing her. "You don't seem as angry as I feel over losing our brother."

"Because when I met Natalia, I realized something. Love is stronger than death. When you love someone, not even death can steal the love you feel for that person. Dreyden and April will always hold a special place in our hearts. We will always have wonderful memories of the times we shared with them. The best way to honor them is to continue to live our lives."

Kellen considered everything his brother said. "Thanks, Ari. I needed to hear that."

"C'mon, let's grab something to eat and maybe catch a game or two."

He rose to his feet. "Sounds like a plan."

Kellen walked alongside Ari but paused to look back at Dreyden's gravestone. "I love you, man," he whispered.

Addison woke to bright sunlight streaming through the gap in the curtains. Fuzzy-headed, she peered at the clock and saw it was nearly ten. She never slept in but clearly her body had needed the rest.

On the empty pillow next to her was a note from Kellen. She picked it up and read it.

At the office getting some work done, but will be back by 11:30 so that we can leave for my parents' house at noon.
Love you,
Kellen

Addison climbed out of bed and padded barefoot to her closet to search for the perfect "meet the future in-laws" outfit. She was nervous and a little bit intimidated. She had great respect for Malcolm and Barbara Alexander, and Addison was pretty sure that she was not who they had in mind for their son.

She decided on a simple black maxi dress and silver sandals. Addison wore her hair down instead of her ponytail.

Staring at her reflection, she placed both hands to her stomach. "We're spending the day with your grandparents, aunts, uncles and cousins. I'm so glad your daddy's going to be there because I'm a little bit scared."

"You don't have to be afraid of my family, sweetheart."

Addison turned around. "When did you get here?"

"Just now," Kellen responded. "You ready to leave?"

She nodded.

Upon their arrival, thirty minutes later, Barbara greeted Addison warmly. "How are you feeling, dear?"

"Much better," she responded. "My doctor's cleared me to go back to work. She said everything is fine with the baby."

"I'm so glad to hear that." Smiling, Barbara placed a hand gently on Addison's stomach. "I can't wait to meet this little bundle of joy."

She relaxed a little. "I'm looking forward to being a mother."

"I know what you mean. My children are my best work." Barbara glanced down at Addison's ring. "Very nice."

"Kellen told you about our engagement?" she asked.

"Yes, he did. Malcolm and I are very happy for you both."

"I was a little worried about how you would take the news," Addison confessed.

"I raised all of my children the very best that I could, and I'm very proud of them. I trust them to know their own minds and hearts." Barbara smiled. "I haven't been disappointed."

"Welcome to our family," Malcolm said, joining them.

Addison glanced over her shoulder at Kellen then back at his parents. "I really hope that I haven't disappointed you."

"You haven't," Malcolm responded. "You can't control who you fall in love with. My wife and I are thrilled to have you as a member of our family." He smiled warmly. "Now, just relax… We won't bite."

Kellen walked up and wrapped his arms around her. "What did I tell you?"

Barbara and Malcolm excused themselves, leaving them alone.

"Feel better now?"

Tension rolling off her in waves, Addison nodded. "Much better."

She met his gaze. "There's something I need to tell you."

"What is it?"

"Dr. Rivers said it was okay if we…"

"Really?"

She nodded.

"Are you sure we won't hurt the baby?"

"We won't."

"We're leaving right after dinner," Kellen announced.

"We most certainly are not," she responded. "We are going to spend time with your family for at least an hour afterward."

"Baby, I love the way you think."

Addison's scent filled the room, clean and floral and utterly captivating. Kellen closed his eyes for a long moment, just breathing in her essence. When he did look at her again, her eyes were warm pools of cocoa, and her lower lip looked full and inviting.

They had been in her condo barely five minutes before Kellen's need to kiss her hit him full force in the pit of his stomach, nearly stealing the breath from his body.

She appeared to be holding her breath, as well.

"You are so beautiful," he whispered.

Kellen stood close enough that he leaned forward and pressed his lips to hers. Gently at first, his lips teased and tormented, until finally she opened her mouth to encourage him to deepen the kiss.

He listened to the song playing in the background. Kellen's lips brushed the shell of her ear as he hummed softly along with the music. "This is our song," he whispered.

"We don't have a song," she responded.

"Maybe we do now."

The tune was a romantic classic about everlasting love found.

Kellen picked her up and carried Addison into the bedroom.

In a matter of minutes, they lay prone in each other's arms, drinking their fill of each other with their mouths. He kissed with a natural mastery that thrilled her.

As Kellen finally pulled his mouth from hers, Addison stroked his chest, loving the feel of his hot skin and beating heart. He moved his mouth down the column of her neck, nipping and teasing with his lips against her sensitive skin. She fought a shiver as she reveled in their skin-to-skin contact.

Hesitant touches became more sure, and their passion grew in intensity, making them both breathless and frantic with need. He moved to the side of her and with a hand, caressed her stomach. "I can't wait to see you grow with my baby."

"Ooh…you're ruining the mood," she said. "Let's discuss my weight gain another time."

"Yes, ma'am," he murmured against her cheek. "I aim to please."

Kellen fell into the soft, sweet taste of her mouth as all other thoughts were driven from his head.

Chapter 22

"Wow! I can't believe that you're getting married."

Addison laughed. "Tia, so much has happened in the last few weeks. I can hardly believe it myself." She held up a wedding gown to her body and stood before a mirror. She and Kellen were getting married in a month, so she didn't have much time to plan the details. "This one's pretty nice."

"I don't think I've seen you this happy in a long time," Tia said. "Apparently, Kellen has turned out to be very good for you. I guess I can say I told you so."

"Although, I'm five years older than he is, but when we're together—it doesn't matter," Addison stated. "We just seem to mesh."

"How did your employees react to the news?"

"That's the interesting part," she said. "Apparently, there were bets as to when we would get together. Everyone said that they saw it coming."

"Will you two continue working together?"

Addison nodded. "For now but I'm actually looking into some other opportunities in-house. I'm not sure it's a good idea to have my husband as my employee. Kellen doesn't think it'll be a problem. I'm not so sure."

"I think that's wise."

She selected another gown. "I like this one."

"That's really nice," Tia told her. "Try that one on."

Addison tried on three more dresses before she returned to the office. She had found one that she liked. Livi Alexander had called Addison earlier to let her know that she had some dresses set aside for her. She wanted to look at those before she made a final decision.

A smile spread across her face. She was getting married.

Addison couldn't be happier.

Addison leaned back against the desk, resting her hips there. Kellen noticed the small roundness forming at her waist and wondered at the tiny life growing inside her.

When he looked up and met her eyes again, she was smiling. It was a smile of contentment, of happiness, of peace.

"She's growing."

"I noticed." Kellen realized she had called the baby "she" and wondered if she had some maternal instinct that told her it was a girl.

"Each day I feel stronger. Each day," she said softly, "I know I'm happy I'm going to be a mother. It's definitely not something I planned or expected to happen, but it is something I can thank you for."

He smiled. "You don't need to thank me—you are the one who is giving me the best gift of my life. I'm so glad God created you and our child just for me. He took my brother, but he gave me something wonderful in return."

Kellen wrapped his arms around her. His breath was warm against her hair.

She shifted her shoulder so she was leaning more against him, the pose both intimate and comfortable.

"Ari told me that love is stronger than death. I understand completely what he meant. I have never felt such an intense emotion. I love you so much."

He'd been awake since four in the morning but had stayed beneath the sheets, thinking. It had nothing to do with habit and everything to do with getting married today.

Getting married to Addison.

"You look a lil' nervous, bro."

Kellen glanced up to find Blaze standing in the doorway of the dressing room. "I'm cool," he responded.

His brother was not convinced. *"Really?"*

"Okay, I'll say it. I'm nervous," Kellen confessed, "but this is huge. I'm getting married to the woman of my dreams."

Blaze laughed as he straightened his younger brother's tie. "I hope you've thrown away your playa card. You certainly don't need it anymore."

"Man, I got rid of it the moment I realized that I'd fallen in love with Addison."

"What are you two talking about?" Ari inquired from the doorway.

"Kellen was just telling me that he's no longer a playa-card-carrying member," Blaze answered.

Ari broke into a light chuckle. "The right woman will do that to you."

Both Blaze and Kellen nodded in agreement.

"The only thing that would really make this day perfect is having Dreyden here," Kellen stated.

"He would have loved to witness your wedding—that's for sure," Blaze commented.

"Yeah," Ari interjected. "Dreyden didn't think you would ever get married."

He laughed. "He wasn't the only one."

They spent time bonding as brothers before Ari and Blaze disappeared to check on their families.

He stared out the window. It was a perfect autumn day for a wedding.

"Kellen, are you all right?"

He turned away from the windows in the dining room to find his parents eyeing him with mild concern.

He smiled and nodded. "I'm fine, Mom."

"Not having second thoughts, are you?" Malcolm asked.

"If I didn't have second thoughts while planning the wedding, Dad, what makes you think I'd have them now?"

His dad shrugged. "Are you truly ready for marriage? I know that you want to do right by Addison because she's pregnant."

"I love her, and I want to marry her." He and Addison had talked at length about getting married, and Kellen was ready. He had the luxury of growing up with parents who loved each other—he wanted the same for his child.

"Did you make Addison aware that there may be some uninvited guests?" his mother inquired.

Kellen knew she was referring to the media. "She expects it, but it's really not at the forefront of our minds."

"Franklin is providing security," Malcolm announced. "No one without an invitation will be able to get in."

"If they do, then I hope they bring a gift or make a donation in my brother's name to the American Cancer Society."

* * *

Her wedding day was absolutely perfect.

Addison woke at 6:00 a.m. She'd retired early the night before; but instead of sleeping in, she got up to help Zaire and Barbara with the final arrangements before it was time to dress in her gown. Quietly she slipped from her bed and to the bathroom.

She ran hot water and washed her face and brushed her teeth before jumping into the shower.

Afterward, she wrapped a thick blue towel around herself and stared in the mirror. Today she was a bride.

Tonight she would be Addison Alexander, Kellen's wife.

She glanced over at the wedding dress hanging on the closet door.

In a few short hours she'd be wearing it, carrying a bouquet of roses and gardenia. It seemed like a wild, crazy dream.

Addison joined her future mother-in-law downstairs.

"How did you sleep?" Barbara asked.

"Well," she responded with a smile. "I slept like a baby."

Glancing around, Addison inquired. "What still needs to be done?"

"Nothing," Barbara told her. "Everything has been taken care of, dear. Today is your big day so we want you to enjoy it. Zaire has arranged for someone to come to the house and style your hair. She also arranged for you to have a…I think she called it a mother-to-be massage."

Addison was touched beyond tears.

"Breakfast is ready," Barbara announced. "Why don't you go get something to eat?"

"Thank you," she murmured.

From the breakfast nook, Addison had a good view of the huge white tent that had been set up for her wedding.

Beautiful floral displays in large vases were placed on either side of the entrance.

She was joined by Livi and Zaire.

"Happy wedding day," Livi said with a smile.

"Thank you," she responded. Addison wiped her mouth with a napkin. "Have either of you seen Kellen this morning?"

"He stayed with Blaze last night," Livi replied.

"Bachelor party?"

Livi nodded. "Only we're not supposed to know they had one."

Everyone in the Alexander family was nice and very friendly. There was warmth and sincerity in their gazes, which made her feel comfortable. Addison felt as if she belonged.

Two hours and a host of pampering later, Addison rose, looked in the mirror and wanted to cry. Her eyes were large and somehow more luminous than she could have imagined, while her skin appeared flawless. Her lips were etched and painted with a color very close to her natural pigment, and her hair was pulled back gently from the sides, the remainder curling simply down her back. A small circle of flowers sat daintily on her head.

At the sound of someone knocking, she said, "Come in."

"It's just me, dear."

"You don't have to knock, Mrs. Alexander."

She gave Addison a tender look. "Call me Mom or Barbara...whichever is more comfortable for you."

Barbara sat down on the leather couch, careful not to wrinkle her navy blue suit. She opened her clutch purse and took out a small box. "This should take care of the borrowed and blue part of wedding tradition."

Addison took the box with shaking fingers. Opening the lid, she found a square velvet box. Inside were nestled a sapphire and diamond necklace and earring set. "Oh, my goodness! They're gorgeous."

"Kellen wanted you to have them for your wedding. It's his hope that if you two have a little girl, she will wear them on the day she gets married."

"He's already starting family traditions." Addison carefully removed the earrings, took out her own pearl studs, which she had planned on wearing, and replaced them with the antique sapphires. The oval stones were surrounded by tiny, winking diamonds.

"Oh, sweetheart, they look stunning on you."

She smiled. "Thank you."

Addison held up the necklace and Barbara fastened it around her neck. "The only thing that could make this day more perfect is having my mother here."

"She's here with you," Barbara said softly. "In your heart."

The time came for Addison to make her grand entrance.

She walked out of the house and was surprised to find her mother's brother waiting for her. "Uncle Elijah…" Addison was overjoyed to have a member of her family present. Her father was an only child and her mother had one brother who never married. "I'm so glad that you're here but how did you know? Everything kind of happened so fast."

"I wouldn't have missed this for the world, honey. Kellen wanted to surprise you, so he gave me a call and told me that it would mean a lot for me to come. He sent a plane and everything."

"I'm sorry for not staying in contact," she said. "I miss Mom so much and…"

He embraced her. "I understand. We have time to catch up later. Right now there's a nice young man waiting for you at the altar. If I don't get you down there to him, I just might be hitchhiking back to Chicago."

She laughed as she looped her arm through his.

Kellen's brows lifted briefly in surprise when she entered the tent, and then a huge smile of approval swept over his face, the heat of it tangible even from several feet away.

Faces turned in her direction, but Addison focused on none other than Kellen and his gray eyes as her shoes silently crushed the grass beneath her feet.

She stopped when he took three steps out of position and lifted his hand, offering it to her.

She took it.

"You look beautiful," he whispered, making her heart swell. He led her under the arch and before the minister, to begin their life together.

Addison's fingers shook in Kellen's hand, her lips quivering as tears trembled on her lashes. She didn't want to cry, but tears flowed as she bubbled up with love and joy as she gazed lovingly at her husband-to-be.

The next ten minutes passed in a haze, a series of impressions that left Addison feeling more and less than she'd expected. The feel of Kellen's hand holding hers, the sound of the minister's voice offering a prayer, handing her bouquet off to Tia so that she could take his fingers in hers.

"You may kiss the bride."

That line came through her consciousness crystal clear, and she lifted startled eyes to Kellen's.

They were warm with understanding and the little secret of the kiss they'd already shared in the weak morning sunlight. Sealed with a kiss… His mouth touched hers, paused, deepened, lingered, until he pulled away just enough that her lips followed ever so briefly. She stared at the fullness of his mouth, smudged with the color of her lipstick, and her cheeks flamed as clapping erupted.

"Ladies and gentlemen," the minister said, gesturing with a hand, "Mr. and Mrs. Kellen Alexander."

Chapter 23

Addison put her hair up in a ponytail, twisting the tail around and around and anchoring the dark bun with a plain band, keeping her neck free and cool. When she was done she placed both hands over the place where her child lay.

Tonight was the first time she'd been alone since her wedding to Kellen a week ago.

She spent the evening planning the menu for tomorrow night's meal, flicking through cookbooks and trying to work out what she could pull together, given the limited supplies in her refrigerator.

Addison settled for a pasta dish—tortellini with salami, goat cheese and Kalamata olives, fresh bread and a baby spinach, Parmesan and pear salad. She made a mental note to go by the grocery store tomorrow after work.

She started prepping for dinner at five o'clock so she could take her time and enjoy the process. She was looking forward to tonight when her husband returned home.

He had flown to Atlanta for a couple of days to check on the young man living in his apartment. There was no point denying it, even to herself—she loved being married to Kellen and missed him in his absence.

Addison had everything prepped by six o'clock, the table set by a quarter past.

In her bedroom she pulled on a loose top made from cashmere and silk, matching it with her steel-gray, wide-legged linen pants. Addison loved the maternity outfit because it was comfortable and made her feel elegant. She felt infinitely better as she slipped on a pair of simple ballet flats and went into the bathroom to do something with her face.

"You look beautiful."

His voice gave her a start because Addison wasn't expecting him home so soon. She turned around and said, "You need to stop sneaking up on me like that."

Kellen walked up to her, planting a kiss on her lips. "I didn't mean to scare you. You take my breath away every time I see you."

He made her feel beautiful in the way his eyes traveled over her lovingly and with endless compliments. Addison wondered if he would be the same way five, ten or fifteen years down the road.

As if he could read her thoughts, he said, "You will always be beautiful to me, sweetheart."

"I feel like the luckiest woman alive," she murmured.

"You are," Kellen responded with a grin.

Addison laughed. "I forget how humble you are."

Kellen refused to relinquish her hand as she started to step away, instead giving it a tug and pulling her back into his arms.

"I need to check on dinner."

"Dinner can wait," he told her.

She looked stunned, and he smiled. Kellen's eyelids drifted closed and he kissed her.

"I missed you," she whispered against his mouth.

"I missed you, too."

Addison freed herself from his grasp. "I really need to check on our dinner, sweetie."

He followed her into the kitchen.

"I'm actually looking forward to going into the office tomorrow," Addison announced as she drained the pasta.

"You're sure you don't want to take another day?" he asked. "We can play hooky tomorrow and just stay in bed."

"While I like that idea, I really think I need to go to work. I've been gone a week."

Kellen took the bowl of pasta out of her hands and laid it on the counter. "Last chance…"

Addison chuckled. "I have a better idea. Why don't we make it an early night? Like right after dinner."

"What can I do to help?" he said with a sexy grin that still made her weak at the knees.

Addison was happy to be back in the office. Although it had only been a couple of weeks, she felt like she'd been away much too long. Smiling, she took her place at the head of the table in the conference room. "Good morning, everyone."

"Good morning, Mrs. Alexander," they replied in unison.

She looked over at Kellen and they shared a laugh.

"Okay," Addison said, resuming her businesslike manner. "What's been going on while we were away? Lee, where are we with the new spa facility in Tennessee?"

"Construction is scheduled to be complete next month."

She nodded in approval. "What about the renovations

of the hotel in Phoenix? I know there were some problems with vandalism. Any updates?"

"We placed more construction advisory bulletins and added barriers," another employee advised. "We also have twenty-four-hour security in the construction zone."

As she discussed some of the new projects, Addison noticed that Kellen seemed unusually quiet. She supposed it had to do with the fact that she didn't assign any of them to him. He was already carrying a stack of projects left over from before their honeymoon trip to Aruba. Addison did not want to overload him.

She could not ignore the unspoken tension between them and was relieved when the meeting was over. She walked straight to her office because she knew that her husband would follow.

Addison had just taken a seat when Kellen burst through the door. "Why didn't you give me one of the new projects?" he asked.

"I didn't want to overwhelm you."

"I can handle the workload," Kellen stated. "I want you to treat me like the rest of the team."

"I don't treat you any different," she argued. "I would've made the same decision with any of my employees, Kellen."

He met her gaze straight on. "I'm not so sure."

She sighed in exasperation. "I'm not going to sit here and argue with you."

"No, you're not because I'm going to my office to do some work. I don't want to give you any more reasons to pass me over for projects."

Kellen frowned, annoyed by the whiny, resentful tone to his own thoughts. Admittedly, Addison probably thought she was doing him a favor. He knew that he needed to learn how to tolerate another person's preferences without getting so bent out of shape, especially where he and Addison were concerned. It was a sure-fire way to make himself and her miserable at work and at home.

He packed up his laptop in his backpack and headed home. Addison had left two hours ago.

The only reason he didn't leave with her was because Kellen could tell that she was still upset with him.

She threw open the front door before he had time to use his key.

They stared at each other.

He didn't know what to say; and as the silence stretched out, he grew more and more uncomfortable.

Addison stood so still, he could barely make out the slight rise and fall of her chest as she breathed. It was like she was waiting to see what he'd say before she decided what to do.

A kiss on the lips seemed presumptuous, so Kellen stuffed his hands into his pockets, instead. Besides, it wouldn't solve a thing.

"I'm sorry," he said.

"I'm sorry, too."

"Can I come inside?"

She broke into a smile as she stepped aside. "It's your home, too."

Kellen pulled her into his arms. "I love you, Addison."

"I know," she murmured. "What happened at work has nothing to do with our love or our marriage. We have to make sure we don't confuse the two."

Addison backed out of his arms. "I really didn't want you overwhelmed with too many projects on your plate. I was just looking out for you."

He agreed. "I made it personal."

"So did I," Addison confessed. "I shouldn't have gotten upset when you came to me."

"It's not going to happen again."

She folded her arms across her chest. "I hope that it won't, because I don't want to keep arguing when it comes to work. I make my decisions based on experience and the strengths of my team."

"I don't want to fight with you, either," he acknowledged. "I especially don't want to upset you while you're carrying our child."

"I don't want to dwell on this anymore." Addison smiled up at him. "While I was waiting on you to come home, I made dinner."

"This is perfect timing because I'm hungry."

"Ooh," she uttered.

Kellen was instantly by her side. "Honey, are you okay?"

Addison's hand drifted to her stomach and rested against the small mound there. His eyes softened as he placed his own hand, strong and warm, on top of hers. The bubble of her belly was firm and taut, and when she opened her eyes, his were shining down at her.

He broke into a grin. "I just felt the baby move."

She closed her eyes at the warmth of his hand seeping through her dress and into her core. "It's such a beautiful feeling."

Kellen gazed tenderly at her. "I love you so much."

She placed a soft kiss on his lips. "I love you, too."

"I can't wait to meet this little one."

Addison nodded in agreement. "You know that our child hears everything we say. I don't want him or her hearing any harsh words between us."

"Our child will always know how much I love you, sweetheart. I will make sure of it."

Chapter 24

"I'm looking forward to seeing your new nephew," Addison told Kellen as she searched through her closet for something to wear. They were spending the day with Zaire and Tyrese to celebrate the birth of the baby.

"He's *our* nephew."

She walked out carrying a maxi dress with an empire waist. "I think he looks just like his father in the pictures Zaire emailed."

Kellen agreed. "He has my sister's mouth, though."

Addison removed her robe, giving him a view of her changing profile.

"You are a beautiful pregnant woman."

She slipped on her dress. "You're such a sweetheart."

Kellen pulled her into his arms. "That's because I love you more than anything else in this world. I thank God for creating you just for me."

Addison planted a kiss on his lips. "I love you, too."

"See, I was right all along," he said with a grin.

"About what?"

"That we belong together."

She laughed. "Oh, I don't know. I think the jury's still out on that one."

"Hey, don't even tease about something like that." He kissed her. "What do you think about selling this place and getting a house?"

"It's something to think about."

Kellen glanced over at the clock on the nightstand. "I guess we need to get going."

"I'm almost ready," Addison said. "I just need to find some shoes and my earrings."

"I'll be in the living room."

An hour later, she was seated in Zaire's family room, laughing and talking with Sage and Livi.

Pushing out of her chair, Addison went to the baby's room in search of Kellen. She found him changing Tai's diaper.

She stopped dead in her tracks and watched. Something about a big, masculine man maneuvering a diaper around the chubby, thrashing legs created an endearing scene.

Kellen looked up at him and grinned, causing her heart to flutter oddly.

"He leaks like a sprinkler system."

Deftly, he smoothed the plastic tabs into place before slipping the tiny legs back into the pajamas.

"I didn't know you were so good with babies."

"Lots of practice."

He lifted the infant in his hands and laid him against a wide, blanket-covered shoulder, patting the tiny back with a tenderness that stirred Addison. One of his hands covered Tai's entire back.

"He's a gorgeous baby," Addison murmured. Seeing

him like this and the way he was around his nieces and nephews, she knew Kellen was going to be a great father.

He was a good man, she knew this. The only problems between them existed at work. There were times when she felt Kellen expected her to choose him because he was her husband. She wondered if any of the other employees thought she was showing favoritism toward Kellen. Addison hoped not because it was not the case. She was grateful that her employees were all accepting.

"What are you thinking about?" Kellen asked, cutting into her thoughts.

She smiled up at him. "Nothing important."

He studied her face. "You're sure?"

Addison gave a slight nod. "Is he asleep?"

"Yes." Kellen took her by the hand. "Let's go join the others. The food should be ready shortly."

He was so sweet and understanding as a husband. Why couldn't he be as understanding when it came to work?

"What is going on with you?" Kellen asked her. "Since we've gotten married, it seems like all you do is find something wrong with my work."

"So you're saying that I'm picking on you," she uttered. Addison was irritated and tense due to the constant arguments between them in the office. Although they had promised one another that they would never bring it home—the last argument ended with Kellen sleeping on the sofa. It was wearing on her emotionally.

"Before we married, I was great, and you trusted me. Now it seems all that has changed."

"The problem is that *you* can't take criticism."

"Neither can you," Kellen shot back.

Addison grabbed her tote. "I'm not doing this again with you. I'm tired, and I'm going home."

"We rode together this morning."

She sent him a sharp glare. Addison silently criticized herself for ever believing that she and Kellen could work together. If their marriage had a chance, she would have to find another solution.

"I'll get my computer and backpack so we can leave."

Addison was silent on the ride home.

"Why don't you sit, and I'll help you with your shoes?" he suggested when they entered the condo.

She looked up at him in surprise. She was still angry with him, but then he flashed her that charming grin of his. Addison walked over to the couch and sat down.

Kellen knelt in front of her to lift her foot.

Eyes locked with hers, he slipped her shoe off, running a lazy circle around her ankle with his thumb.

Addison watched, breathless, as his large hands massaged her foot.

So unbelievably sexy.

"Okay?"

"Perfect." Flustered, Addison cleared her throat, clearly working to maintain her poise.

He picked up her other foot, giving it the same attention as the first. Kellen let his hands skim up over her calves, stroking a light path behind her knees as he went on.

"You drive me so crazy," she murmured. "I love you but when we're in the office, there are days that I really don't like you."

"It just seems that things have changed since we got married."

"They haven't," Addison stated. "I think that maybe your expectations changed."

Kellen shook his head in denial. "This is my passion. Surely you understand this."

"I do understand, but I need you to know that I have years of experience as an engineer and a manager. I do know what I'm doing." She paused for a moment before adding, "I think the team feels the tension between us in the office. This is what I didn't want to happen, Kellen."

"I speak my mind. You know that."

"If we continue to have problems working together, then I'm going to have to make some changes."

He met her gaze.

"What do you mean by that?"

"We will have to make some changes," she stated. "I'm not going to have our issues the subject of water-cooler gossip."

"You need to stop worrying about what others think."

"And you need to learn how to be a team player."

"Kellen, there's a position in Seattle that I was of-fered, and I've been thinking about taking it," Addison announced over breakfast. "I think that it would be bet-ter for our marriage if we don't have to work together on a daily basis."

"The only problem is that I'm not interested in moving to Seattle," Kellen responded. "I love living here in Los Angeles." He was surprised by Addison's announcement. He thought things between them were getting better. They still disagreed from time to time, but not as much lately.

"You wouldn't have to move," she responded. "I'd get an apartment there and come home on the weekends."

Kellen met her gaze straight on. "Addison, what about our child?" He couldn't believe she was thinking of tak-ing their child and living in Seattle without him.

"The baby would be with me, of course."

"I don't think so," he uttered. "You're my wife, and I intend to be a full-time father to my child. Taking a job in Seattle is just not an option."

She sighed in resignation. "I don't know what else to do, Kellen. It's clear that we can't work together because it's affecting our marriage. Half the time we come home and we don't talk to each other. I love you, but I don't want to live this way."

"You could be a full-time mother," he suggested. "You don't have to work."

"We've had this discussion before. I enjoy what I do, and I intend to keep working," Addison told him.

"You don't know how you're going to feel until after the baby gets here," Kellen stated. "You may change your mind. Natalia isn't working more than two or three days a week since she had the twins."

She shook her head. "I doubt it."

He finished off his coffee. "Well, I don't want you and the baby traveling back and forth from Seattle to Los Angeles. We'll work this out."

"I hate arguing with you, Kellen. When we disagree at work it travels over into our home life. I can't do this anymore."

Kellen reached across the table, taking her hand into his. "I don't want you stressed out. I'll do whatever I have to do to keep you happy at work and at home. I promise."

They made small talk during the drive to the office. He was worried about losing his family. In truth, Kellen was scared. Something had to be done if his wife was considering moving all the way to Seattle.

"I've been thinking," Kellen said as he sat down in one of the visitor chairs in Addison's office. "There's an opening in Blaze's department. I'm going to talk to him about it."

"Sales and marketing? Is this something you really want to do?" she asked.

"I am willing to do whatever it takes to save my marriage," Kellen answered. "You and our child are more important to me than any job."

"You would really do this for us?"

"I love you, Addison. More than I have ever loved anyone, and I'm not going to lose you."

"I love you, too, but I just don't think you're going to like being in sales and marketing," she stated. "This is what you love doing. Look, I don't have to go to Seattle. I'm sure I can find something here in Los Angeles."

He shrugged in nonchalance. "I'm not going to have you leave ADDG. I wouldn't do this to my father."

"Are you really sure about this?" she asked, pushing away from her desk.

Kellen nodded as he rose to his feet. "You and our child are important to me, and I can't risk losing you. I'm going to talk to Blaze about it tomorrow."

She looked as if she were seeing him with new eyes. "I can't believe you're willing to sacrifice your own happiness like this."

After a moment he added, "I will be happy in any job that will help me keep my family together."

Chapter 25

"Did I just hear you correctly?" Blaze asked. "Did you just say you want to work in sales?"

Kellen nodded. "Addison and I have decided that it's not such a good idea to work together."

"Having trouble separating your work lives from your personal?"

"Something like that," he uttered. "I love her so much, Blaze. I don't want to lose her."

Blaze sat up straight in his chair. "Things okay between you two?"

"Yeah. It's just that she's pregnant and I don't want anything to stress her out. Her pregnancy is high risk, so it's important that Addison stays calm." He paused for a moment and then said, "We've been arguing a lot at work."

"All you've ever wanted to do was architectural engineering, Kellen. Have you considered working for another firm?"

"I want to stay in the family business. Addison was offered a job in Seattle, but that's definitely not an option. She offered to leave ADDG, but I think Dad would probably kill me."

Blaze nodded in agreement.

"You know I have sales experience. Remember when I worked at the car dealership while I was in undergrad?"

His brother broke into a grin. "I do remember that. However, this is very different from selling cars."

"I can sell sugar to a salt dealer and you know it."

Blaze laughed. "You're right about that."

"I have to do this," Kellen stated. "I am not going to lose my wife."

"I admire your dedication to Addison and your child, little brother. If you want the job—it's yours."

He smiled. "Thanks."

Kellen stood outside his brother's office. He had just given up his career for the woman he loved. What he felt was anything but relief.

Addison knew that Kellen wasn't happy with his new job and planned to talk to him once she arrived home. He was usually home before her.

He had cooked dinner for them.

"Something smells delicious," she said when she entered the condo.

Kellen greeted her with a kiss. "I hope it tastes good. I made roast chicken."

"How was your day?" she inquired.

"It was okay," he responded. "How was yours?"

"Good," Addison replied. "We just got this new project..." Her voice died at the expression on Kellen's face. "Let's not talk about work."

He didn't respond.

"I'm going to change into something comfortable."

"Dinner will be on the table by the time you come back," Kellen told her.

When she returned ten minutes later, Addison sat in the chair he held out for her. "Thanks, sweetie."

She noted that he was unusually quiet during dinner. Addison wiped her mouth on the edge of her napkin and said, "I know that you are not going to like this, but I really think I should leave ADDG. I don't think it'll be hard for me to land a position somewhere else."

Kellen shook his head. "No, I don't like that idea at all."

"You don't want me to take the position in Seattle. You don't want me working for someone else at all. Our marriage is suffering. What do you want me to do?" She hated seeing him look so miserable, although he was trying hard not to show it.

"Try having some faith in me," Kellen responded. "I can do this. Working in sales isn't all bad."

She wiped away a lone tear. "But I can tell that you hate it. Honey, it's written all over your face."

"I'm not crazy about the job, but I wouldn't exactly say that I hate it."

"I know you," Addison stated. "You don't like this sales position at all."

She shifted in her chair. At eight and a half months pregnant, it was difficult to find a comfortable position.

"The baby is almost here," Kellen said. "You'll be on maternity leave and I'm taking some time off, too—we can talk about our next steps."

"I want you to know that your happiness is very important to me, Kellen. I worry that you're going to resent me."

"I'm not going to resent you, sweetheart."

Groaning, Addison suddenly doubled over.

"What's wrong?"

"That was a strong kick…" she said, although she wasn't really sure what it was. "I think that's what it was."

Kellen pushed away from the table. "Was it a contraction?"

"I don't know."

Addison was fine one minute, and then the next minute, she was moaning. "Oooh…"

Kellen helped her up from the table. "I don't think the baby's kicking. You're having contractions."

Intense contractions hit her in a single wave.

She doubled over once again while he rubbed her back.

Before Addison realized it, she was on all fours, moaning. She'd had some back pain off and on throughout the day, but what she was feeling now was agony. She'd had no idea contractions were this painful.

After the next wave Addison managed to get out the words, "Call ambulance."

"I can take you to the hospital."

She shook her head. She was hurting too much to speak.

"Water…" Addison muttered after a moment. "Water broke."

"You're in labor," Kellen said. "I need to get you to the hospital."

"It's too late," she panted.

He looked at her in confusion. "What do you mean it's too late?"

"The baby's coming."

Kellen called 9-1-1. "My wife is in labor and we need help. Get someone over here quick, please."

"Sir, I need you to listen to me, okay? I want you to support the shoulders and hold the hips and legs firmly. Remember the baby will be slippery, so don't drop it, okay?"

Kellen said a quick prayer as he reached in, palms facing up, prompting a moan from Addison. "It's going to be okay, honey."

He slowly guided the baby out, while trying to keep Addison calm and listening to the operator.

"You're doing great, sweetheart," he encouraged.

When Kellen saw that the umbilical cord was snaked around the baby's neck, tightly, his heart started pounding even faster, and his adrenaline went from overdrive to supersonic.

The baby's eyes were shut and Kellen saw no sign of breathing.

"Wrap the baby in a clean cloth or towel…tie a shoelace tightly around the umbilical cord…"

He stopped listening to her. Kellen was focused on the neck. "Oh, my God, the baby's not breathing," he said. "Breathe, baby, breathe."

Somewhere in the depths of his mind, he heard Addison crying.

"The cord is around the baby's neck. What do I do? *What do I do?"*

"Don't tie the umbilical cord just yet," the operator advised. "The paramedics should be arriving any moment. Carefully unravel the cord from around the neck."

"My baby…" Addison moaned. "Nooo…"

Kellen placed the baby down on the towel after he removed the cord from around her neck. The baby was so fragile with a small, purplish-reddish body.

"Let me give you CPR instructions," the operator offered.

Miraculously, after he stroked the baby gently a couple of times, she opened her eyes, began to breathe and move.

That moment—the eyes opening—was not about joy or a celestial choir suddenly singing from heaven. It was hope. Kellen had hoped that his baby would live. It was something he thought died with Dreyden.

The baby started to cry.

He had never heard anything so wonderful as his daughter's first cry.

Kellen used a shoelace to tie off the cord just as the paramedics arrived.

He handed the baby to Addison and ran to the door to let the paramedics in.

While they tended to his wife, Kellen held his baby daughter.

Delivering his own child was an incredible experience—the experience of a lifetime. Kellen felt as if he now had a unique connection to his daughter. It was one that he would feel throughout his life. The first sound his daughter heard upon emerging from her mother's womb was her father praying and begging her to breathe.

For him, it reinforced the powerful feeling that all fathers wanted for their families—the feeling and security that they will take care of them, protect them and provide for them.

Professionally, it was easy to get lost in his ambition, Kellen realized, but in that moment of delivering his daughter, the game of life called *success* no longer existed. Having a child wasn't part of that game. It was something real, immediate and primal, the very stuff of what actually mattered—love.

Chapter 26

From the living room she heard Kieran's baby voice and Kellen's manly one. He was giving his daughter a sponge bath in front of the fireplace. The diapered baby lay on a quilt, tiny legs and arms bicycling for all she was worth. Her round face was alive with interest as Kellen, on his knees beside her, carried on a one-sided conversation.

"Are you Daddy's angel girl?" he asked, leaning over her.

Kieran cooed in response and slammed one little fist against the side of his face.

Kellen laughed and nuzzled the rounded belly, an action that sent Kieran's arms and legs into fast motion. Suddenly, he scooped the child into his hands and lifted her overhead, waggling her gently from side to side.

Kieran's toothless mouth spread wide, and a delighted gurgle filled the dimly lit living room.

Addison felt a catch beneath her ribs at the pleasure father and daughter found in one another. There was something beautiful and pure in that kind of love.

Tears pricked at her eyelids. A deep, tearing need took her breath, and she turned back toward the bedroom.

When she returned to the living room, Kieran was dressed in red footed pajamas, her face shiny from the bath and her dark hair neatly smoothed. Cradled in Kellen's arms, eyes wide and earnest, she eagerly sucked down her supper.

Addison settled into the easy chair opposite Kellen's, curling her legs beneath her. "You're a good father."

It was true. She'd rarely seen a man so attuned to his child.

"I'm trying." Kellen slid the empty bottle from the baby's mouth and lifted her against his shoulder for burping. "I made a lot of stupid mistakes before Kieran came along, but I want to be a better man for her and for you."

Tiptoeing, Addison made her way to the bassinet in the center of the floor. A Winnie-the-Pooh nightlight provided just enough illumination for her to make out the tiny baby stirring in the crib.

Kieran.

As always, her heart melted at the sight of her beautiful two-month-old daughter.

How did I ever get so lucky?

What had been a scary, unplanned pregnancy turned into the greatest joy of her life. Not a day passed that Addison didn't thank her lucky stars.

"Hey, there, honey bear." She bent and reached into the crib.

Lifting Kieran, she put the baby to her shoulder, kissing a crown of soft, curly hair as she did.

"Are you hungry?"

In response, Kieran wiggled and mewed and made sucking noises with her tiny mouth.

"Let's go, then. Why don't we visit with Daddy while you eat? What do you say about that?"

Kieran wiggled some more, snuggling close.

Addison walked down the hall to the office she shared with Kellen.

He looked up and smiled when they entered. "What's going on with you two?"

"I brought your daughter in here to spend some time with you while she has her bottle."

Kellen pushed away from his desk. "If you don't mind, I'd like to feed her. I'll wash my hands and be right back."

"Grab her bottle off the counter," she told him.

Addison sat down in the overstuffed leather chair and swiveled to face the window. Kieran was a good baby, a blessing from heaven.

Kieran gave a fussy cry.

"Daddy's coming, sweetie."

"I have it right here," Kellen said as he walked briskly into the room.

He picked up the baby and carried her back to his seat behind the desk.

Kieran sucked greedily, prompting laughter from her parents.

Balancing Kieran in his lap, Kellen rubbed the baby's back and waited for a burp.

When the infant showed no more interest in her bottle, he sat it down on the desk. "I guess she's full."

"She looks so content in your arms," Addison stated. "I can tell that she loves her daddy. She just lights up whenever she hears your voice."

"I'm crazy about her," he responded with a smile. "I never knew I could love someone so much." Kellen raised his gaze to look at her. "Addison, you and Kieran are the two most important people in my life. I don't want to lose you."

"I know that you're unhappy, Kellen."

"Let's not do this again," he said. "I don't want you and my daughter living in Seattle."

"I'm not going anywhere," Addison interjected quickly. "That's not what this is about. Kellen, I talked to your father and he agrees with me. I think we've found the perfect solution."

"Am I getting fired again?"

She smiled up at him. "More like a promotion."

"To what?" he asked.

"You are perfect for a newly created position in Mike's department. It's an intermediate design architect position. You will specialize in hotel projects in all design stages."

"Really?"

She nodded. "It's perfect for you."

"I think so, too, but what does my dad think?"

"He agrees with me," Addison responded. "Honey, your father has a lot of faith in you. *I have* faith in you."

Kellen rose to his feet and walked around the desk to where she sat. He bent down and placed the baby in her arms before kissing her. "You did this for me?"

"It was either that or quit working, and I don't want to do that," she confessed. "I love our daughter, but I don't just want to be a mother. I want my career, as well."

"I understand that," Kellen responded. "I would never ask you to give up your job."

"Will you feel this way if we have more children?" Addison questioned.

"Even then," he answered as he leaned against the edge of his desk.

She planted a kiss on the baby's forehead. "Actually, I've been thinking that it would be nice to have on-site child-care facilities for the staff. I never realized how much mothers sacrifice when working until now. At least with child-care on-site, they can spend breaks with their children every day."

He smiled. "I like that idea. You should put together a proposal and submit it to Dad."

"I think I will."

After she settled a sleeping Kieran in her crib an hour later, Addison stopped in her tracks in the doorway, pulled up by the sight of her husband sitting on the edge of the bed. "What are you doing in here?" she asked. "I thought I left you in the office working."

"I figured since Kieran is sleeping, we might as well take a nap, too."

Addison broke into a grin. "Are you sure napping is what you have in mind?"

"Come to bed, wife. Whatever happens after that..."

In his gaze was a promise of forever...and happily ever after.

* * * * *

REQUEST YOUR FREE BOOKS!

2 FREE NOVELS
PLUS 2 *FREE GIFTS!*

KIMANI™
ROMANCE

Love's ultimate destination!

Every passion has a price...

AFTER HOURS

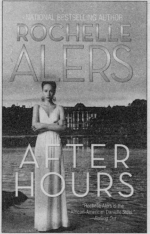

National Bestselling Author

ROCHELLE ALERS

Adina's beauty and wiles have enabled her to adopt the fast-paced lifestyle of the rich and fabulous...until she learns there's a contract out on her life. She flees Brooklyn to start over in an upscale suburb, living among those she's always envied. There she meets Sybil, a secret dominatrix, and Karla, whose need for male attention is spiraling out of control.

As Adina is drawn into the sizzling reality beyond her new friends' perfect facades, she is also hiding her own not-so-innocent past. Now each woman is about to discover that some secrets are simply impossible to keep hidden.

"Fast-paced and well-written."
—*RT Book Reviews* on *AFTER HOURS*

Available June 2014 wherever books are sold!

HARLEQUIN®
www.Harlequin.com

KPRA1450614

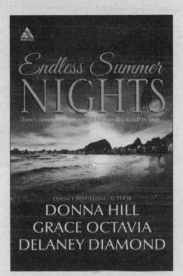

If she's going to win,
she needs to play
the game…

Pamela Yaye

Newscaster Angela Kelly wants to take the Windy City by storm. But with her show's low ratings, she stands to lose everything. An exposé on professional baseball player Demetri Morretti might be her last shot. But when Angela finds herself in danger, Demetri will have to prove there's more to him than just his playboy status….

"A page-turner from start to finish…a great story."
—*RT Book Reviews* on *GAMES OF THE HEART*

The Morretti Millionaires

Has she fallen for an innocent man...or a guilty one?

KIMANI ROMANCE

KIMANI
HOT
PROMISE ME FOREVER

WHEN MORNING COMES

WHEN MORNING COMES

HARMONY EVANS

HARMONY EVANS

Autumn Hilliard's fine mind and natural beauty are the reasons she's an excellent private detective. But investment banker Isaac Mason is nothing like the men Autumn has investigated in the past. Working her way into Isaac's world, she hopes to prove his innocence. Otherwise Autumn may pay the ultimate price for giving her trust—and her heart—to the wrong man....

Available July 2014
wherever books are sold!

H HARLEQUIN®
www.Harlequin.com

KPHE3630714

He needs her help…
and wants her heart.

KIMANI ROMANCE

MIDNIGHT
Play

THE BLUE DYNASTY

Lisa Marie Perry

MIDNIGHT
Play

Lisa Marie Perry

As general manager of the Las Vegas Slayers, Danica Blue often goes toe-to-toe with players with colossal egos. Quarterback Dex Harper has a hell-raiser reputation that he insists he doesn't deserve. To save his career he needs Danica's PR savvy, but once he discovers the real woman behind that flawless facade, he realizes how much his job *and* his heart are at stake.

THE BLUE DYNASTY

Available July 2014
wherever books are sold!

HARLEQUIN®
www.Harlequin.com

KPLMP3640714